Misgivings

To order additional copies, please contact us.
BookSurge, LLC
www.booksurge.com
1-866-308-6235
orders@booksurge.com

Misgivings

Robert Calsin

2006

Misgivings

For my mom and dad, Elizabeth and Hank--their example was priceless. For my children, Katy and Mike--a father couldn't be more blessed. And for my wife, Mary--my loving partner and best friend.

CHAPTER 1

The hot humid room was dimly lit, with a solitary lamp hanging above the large round table. A small rotating fan purred, causing the curtain of beads at the doorway to click against one another, routinely adding to the eerie atmosphere. Incense permeated the air.

Madam Therese was beginning to mentally connect with her new client, who was sitting across the table. It was the summer of 1980, and she was a psychic fixture in Miami, serving her clients for over twenty-five years. He had told her that he was a real estate developer. He was struggling—she could see it in his eyes.

"Mr. Larson, tell me about your concerns."

He leaned forward. His face was wet with perspiration, and he looked at her with piercing eyes.

"I must know what my future will bring. Will I achieve success? And if so, when?"

Madam Therese concentrated her energies, her eyes glistening. She was silent as she looked down at her Tarot cards, the shadows in the room partially covering her face. She shuffled and divided the deck into three facedown piles. She turned up the card on the top of each pile, gazing at her mystical tools. Her eyes closed for several minutes, again in silence. They slowly opened, and she began to speak.

"The cards tell me a great deal about your past and your future, Mr. Larson. The first card is the 'Knight of Wands.' It tells me that you have been unhappy about your finances and your business in general. Many people haven't been straightforward with you. They have promised you much, but have given you nothing."

He was visibly amazed at her insight, moving closer to the table.

"That's right—the bankers. They promised to give my partner and me the funds necessary for our projects, but they haven't."

"I see that," She responded, closing her eyes and nodding her head in agreement.

"What else do you see, Madam Therese?" he asked, almost begging.

"'Strength' is your second card—it is powerful, and tells us much about your near future."

He sat and listened, trancelike.

"Your business life will change. You will be rewarded for your persistence and effort. Your financial troubles will be handled effectively. Promises will be fulfilled and all your debts will be paid," She responded with a slight smile.

He leaned back in his chair and took a deep breath.

Again she closed her eyes.

"But..."

"But what?" He asked, pulling himself back to the table and into her sphere.

Opening her eyes, she looked at him. Her expression was stoic.

"A situation will arise with one who will exert a great deal of power or influence over you, but you must be steadfast in your goals. When challenged, you must take up the gauntlet and win. You must not allow anything or anyone to stand in your way!"

His expression mirrored hers.

"I will not," He responded with finality.

"And what does the third card tell you?" He continued.

She nodded her head slowly.

"The answer is indicated in the 'Ace of Pentacles.' If you persevere, your world will be transformed, and you will have great wealth," She answered, again with a slight smile.

"When?"

"The card tells me soon." Her smile quickly disappeared, and she continued, "But, I must remind you, your opponent will have great power."

His face was taut and his gaze was unwavering.

"No one will prevent me from reaching my true destiny. No one."

It was an hour before sunrise, and Bill Casey was on the third of his daily five-mile run. Part of his regimentation was listening to music. Today, it was James Taylor singing, "You've Got a Friend."

I don't think so, James—at least not at the office, Bill thought.

The sweat was pouring off his body, and his shorts and shirt looked as though he had just stepped out of the shower. The salt was stinging his eyes, even though he continually wiped his head and face with a towel that he kept hanging from his fanny pack.

I know, it's June in south Florida, Bill thought, *but it's also five o'clock in the morning, for God's sake. I don't think I'll ever get used to this heat and humidity—it's like carrying another fifty pounds.*

He rounded the corner and started on his final stretch. Picking up speed in the last quarter mile, his face tightened, and his arms and legs moved like a finely tuned machine, set on high. He continued slightly past his marker, and then gradually slowed his pace. Bill's cool—down was a short walk back to his house in the Land of the Presidents, a beautiful West Palm Beach neighborhood with a golf course running along one side and Lake Mangonia on the other. Palm trees and other tropical foliage of all varieties were everywhere.

He ate his regular breakfast of fruit and juice, had a quick shower, and left for his office in Palm Beach.

Later that morning, he walked into the second session of a financial management seminar at the Boca Raton Resort and Club just as it was ending. He passed two of the attendees who were leaving.

"That young son-of-a-bitch doesn't know his ass from a hole in the ground," one of them growled to his companion.

"He's got some nerve, acting as cocky as he does. I can't wait to see him screw up."

The conversation continued as they walked to a hospitality table nearby for a cup of coffee.

Those are the liveliest reactions I've ever heard at these meetings, Bill thought, smiling. *The presenter must not be a good 'ole boy.*

He walked up to the speakers' table and looked at the name card: RON JAMESON/DAWN SAVINGS ASSOCIATION. He turned. There were several people conversing in small groups, and a few individuals getting their handouts together so they could leave for the next session. He noticed a friend he'd met through a trade organization, who was also one of Dawn's senior officers. They had been active together on several committees and had realized that their philosophies, as far as the industry was concerned, were similar. Bill waved and approached him.

Nick was underweight, almost pallid looking, but always

appeared to have the energy of ten people—it seemed to emanate from a spirit within. He was extremely animated, and with his body often moving in several different directions at once, he always looked disheveled. His shirt had a habit of partially hanging out of his pants, and his hair never seemed to lay right. On the other hand, he was intelligent—very knowledgeable about almost any subject discussed.

"I'm sorry I missed the session. It sounds like it was interesting. Unfortunately, I had some deadlines to meet."

"Well, it certainly ended up being mildly controversial," Nick replied, raising his eyebrows.

Bill smiled. "From some of the comments I heard, it sounds like *mildly* is a gross understatement."

"Well, you know how those old-timers are—they're cynical of new ideas, no matter how logical. The critics are the same people making long-term fixed rate mortgages with short-term deposits, and holding them," He said, shaking his head.

"Short-sighted."

"No question about it. And Dawn has so much potential, it's mind-boggling. There's really no competition!" He said, raising his hands.

"And Ron doesn't even mind telling everyone exactly what we do to make money and grow. He feels that by the time they understand and implement, if that happens, we'll be so far ahead in the ball game, they'll never catch up."

Bill noticed that when Nick spoke about Dawn, his eyes glistened. *This guy is totally consumed*, he thought.

"How about introducing me to Ron?"

"No problem. He's just finishing up with a few of the attendees that have open minds."

They walked over to the dais.

Bill watched Ron as he ended his post-session conversations. He was a slight man with a youthful face. His prematurely gray hair made him look somewhat older, and he exuded confidence.

"Ron, I'd like you to meet Bill Casey."

Ron smiled at Bill and walked down the steps of the portable stage.

"I've been looking forward to our meeting. Nick has been very complimentary in his comments about you."

"Well, the pleasure's mine, and I feel the same way about him. He's a tremendous asset to your organization."

"Thanks. You must have met each other at a Mutual Admiration Society meeting," he quipped. "Were you here for the session?"

"No, I missed it, but I heard some interesting comments on the way in," Bill said, waiting to see Ron's reaction.

Ron grinned and shook his head. "It's amazing what these people could do, but refuse. They're in a rut they'll never get out of—and that's fine. They have the opportunity, but they're not taking advantage of it, so we'll prosper."

Ron looked at his watch. "I have to run," he continued, putting his hand on Bill's shoulder, "but Nick and I would like to get together with you. We have a proposition we think you'll be interested in. I'm out of town next week—how about breakfast near the middle of the month?"

"Sure, I'd enjoy that."

"Nick will call you and set something up."

"Great."

Bill walked into Mom's Family Restaurant on Military Trail. The pleasant aroma of freshly brewed coffee, bacon,

and pancakes sweetened the air. He saw Nick and Ron at a
far corner table.

"Gentlemen," He said, extending his hand as he walked
up to the table.

Both men stood and greeted Bill warmly.

"Glad you could make it," Ron said, as they sat down.

"We've actually been trying to get together with you for
the last couple of months, but we couldn't even coordinate
a date among ourselves," Nick said, laughing. "Things are
crazy at Dawn."

They ordered, ate, and discussed the potential of the
banking business between bites.

Ron glanced at a clock on the wall. "Time's getting away
from me," He said. "Listen, Bill—we'd like you to come to
work for us."

Bill almost choked on his pancake.

Before he could respond, Ron continued. "I'm not
looking for an answer now; I'd just like you to think about
the possibilities. Palm Savings isn't going anywhere. I don't
think John and the boys over there have had an original
idea in years. I know Palm is ten times the size of Dawn,
but our growth is phenomenal, and you've probably heard
from Nick that we're diversified and exciting."

Ron and Nick both looked at Bill, and there was a short
silence.

"I don't know what to say," Bill finally responded.

"This is really a shock. When you invited me here, I
really thought that you wanted to broach the subject of
a possible collaboration of some sort between our two
organizations."

"That would never happen," Ron said. "I have no respect
for anyone there except for you. They're nice people, but
Palm is a microcosm of what's wrong with the savings and
loan industry."

Bill looked at Ron quizzically. "What position are you trying to fill?" he asked. Without waiting for an answer, he continued, "You've got a chief financial officer," looking over at Nick.

"Well, our chief lending officer isn't working out, and Nick wants to give it a shot. If we make that change, we'll need a CFO."

Before Bill could answer, Ron held up his hand. "I know what you're thinking. How can this guy afford to pay me what I'm making now, or more importantly, what I'm worth?"

"I haven't had a chance to think about that yet," Bill responded.

"You would have, if I gave you more time. The answer is, I can't. Not what you're worth, that is. But I have a copy of the Palm Savings proxy, and I know we can pay what they are. Hopefully, that would only be temporary. We really believe that you have great potential with Dawn."

"How long do I have to think about your offer?"

"Can you let me know by the end of the week?"

"Sure," Bill responded, hesitantly. "Listen, I'm going to have to excuse myself. I have a meeting in a half hour back at the office."

"That's fine," Ron said, as he stood up. "We have to get back, too. Please think about this seriously. Don't make me take second-best."

"Honey, can we talk for a few minutes?" Bill asked, as he and Marie walked toward the family room after putting Beth and Christopher to bed.

She looked back at him, smiling.

"This sounds like a serious conversation, Mr. Casey."

He put his arm around her as they sat down.

"Well, it is."

"Go on," She said, her smile fading.

"I want to leave Palm Savings."

"Bill," She said, turning abruptly toward him, "I don't believe this. How many times have we discussed this before?"

"I know, I know," Bill responded, taking her hands in his. "But the situation there continues to deteriorate, and there's another twist. Dawn Savings has offered me a position."

"Why is Dawn familiar? Who do we know that works there?"

"Nick Donofrio."

She pulled her hands away from Bill's grasp and adjusted herself on the couch.

"Is Nick leaving?"

"No, but he's being moved to another position, and the CFO's slot is open."

Marie looked down at her lap, but said nothing.

"I talked with Nick and Ron Jameson, the president, this morning. Their philosophy and mine, as far as the future of this industry, match almost exactly."

Marie looked up. "How long have they been in business? It can't be that big a company. I haven't seen that many branches around town."

"Two years and two branches," He said, with a blank expression on his face.

"Oh, Bill," Marie responded, combing her hair back away from her face with her fingers, avoiding Bill's eyes.

"Palm's been in business forever, and they have branches everywhere."

"I understand that, but the company's in trouble. John and the board just haven't admitted it yet."

Bill lifted Marie's chin with his hand and looked into her eyes.

"I have to go somewhere—there's no future at Palm—and I might as well join a company that has some positive direction."

Marie got up and started to walk toward their bedroom. She turned back and looked at Bill.

"What are they offering you?"

"My current salary."

"So, you're considering accepting a CFO's position with a very small company that's only been in business two years, with no increase in pay. The risk for you and your family sounds pretty large when you consider where you're coming from."

"I realize it's a gamble, but there's also a tremendous risk if I stay at Palm."

She shook her head, turned, and walked slowly into the bedroom, closing the door.

Bill walked into John Conniston's office. His blinds were closed and it was dark, except for the leaded glass lamp above his cluttered desk.

I really care for this guy, Bill thought, *but he's just too set in his ways.*

John was evidently trying to read a memo he had in his hands, but he didn't appear to be in complete control of his ability to sit erect. He was in that semi-conscious state, somewhere between being awake and asleep. His reading glasses were farther down the bridge of his nose than they should have been, and his head was bobbing, falling lower and lower, dangerously close to meeting the top of the desk.

Bill cleared his throat, and John's body jerked upright. He straightened his glasses and looked up at his visitor.

"Bill," He said, hesitating, still obviously trying to get his bearings. "Did we have an appointment?"

"No, but can I have a few minutes of your time?" Bill said, as he sat down in one of the guest chairs.

John looked at his watch. "Sure, what can I do for you?"

"I'm leaving Palm Savings."

John sat up even straighter, squinting at Bill with a questioning face. "You're doing what, Bill?"

"I'm leaving Palm."

"But why?" Before Bill could answer, John continued.

"Are you still questioning our direction—I thought I convinced you that everything was going to be okay."

"No, you didn't convince me—I gave up trying to convince you that we're headed the wrong way down a one-way street. As an executive vice president of this company, I can't sit by and watch Palm commit financial suicide."

Bill got up and started to pace as he talked.

"We continue to borrow short with savings accounts and certificates of deposits, and lend long in mortgages. Interest rates are all over the board and we're going to lose our ass."

"But, Bill," John said, almost pleading, "let me explain again. I think..."

Bill held up his hand. "Wait, John, I don't want to talk about our differing points of view. There's nothing new. We're at two opposite ends of the spectrum. I can tell you at least six or seven horror stories of companies just like ours who have gone under this past year."

Bill stopped talking, looked up at the blank ceiling trying to clear his head and then focused back on John.

"Uncle Sam is not going to bail us out," he continued

quietly. "I'll stay until you get a replacement, but I am going."

"Where?"

"Dawn Savings."

John took his glasses off and rubbed his eyes. He crossed his arms on his desk and looked directly at Bill. "I'd advise against a move to that company. Those boys are dangerous."

"They've done fine up to now, and I have respect for what they're trying to build."

"Too risk-orientated," John responded, shaking his head, his eyes closed in apparent disappointment over what he was hearing. "They're into those acquisition, development and construction packages with less than desirable borrowers. It's not safe for the business, or for you, for that matter."

"Maybe so, but I feel that continuing on our current course, hoping the government and regulators will save us, is a mistake."

"I'll call our auditors and an executive search firm tomorrow morning and see if they have any potential candidates for my position."

He began to leave.

"Bill."

"Yeah, John."

"You've got a good head on your shoulders, and you've made some good career moves up till now. Don't ruin it."

"I appreciate your advice, John, but I'm going with Dawn," Bill said, forcing a smile and continuing out of the office.

CHAPTER 2

Bill parked his car in a relatively plain strip shopping center in West Palm Beach and entered one of the nearby storefronts. As he walked through the door into a reception area, he heard an eclectic mixture of sounds: multiple conversations, telephones ringing, machines humming and clicking. He hesitated as he looked into the small lobby, and noticed that everyone—employees and customers—appeared pleased to be there.

A young woman with a brilliant smile was seated at the front desk. She popped out of her chair and held out her hand to greet him.

"Welcome to Dawn Savings. May I help you please?"

"Yes. I have an appointment to see Ron Jameson. My name is Bill Casey."

"Please have a seat. I'll let him know you're here."

Bill picked up the Wall Street Journal and started reading an article about high-yield bonds.

"Bill, I'm Lydia Lewis," a friendly looking stranger said, as she walked into the lobby. "Ron will be tied up for the next few minutes and he asked me to introduce myself, give you some background and a little tour."

"Great, it's a pleasure to meet you."

"Well," Lydia said smiling, "let's begin by going to one of the strangest places you've ever been."

"I'm not sure what you mean by that, but I'm sure I'll find out soon," Bill said.

Lydia turned and winked. "Yes, you will."

They walked past the teller area, through loan servicing,

and into another connected storefront that was a maze of partitions and a hive of activity. They sat down at a desk and side chair at the edge of the action.

Bill looked around. *This is Florida, and it looks like Manhattan at 42nd and Madison during lunch hour*, he thought.

"It appears as though you've outgrown the office."

"That happened the day we moved in. I think that's good, don't you?"

"It could be," Bill said, smiling. "What's your background?"

"Well, I've had no banking whatsoever. I was previously employed at one of the state mental facilities—Ron felt I was perfect for Dawn," She said, laughing.

"I love working with people. Trying to understand and please the customers is something bankers and thrift people haven't spent much time doing. I know this may sound a little trite, but our customers do come first.

"And they should," Bill said.

"Financial institutions are pretty much vanilla, so Dawn has to be somewhat different to survive and prosper," Lydia continued. "We have regional focus groups, community rooms that are used almost every day, and a 'retail' mentality."

She hesitated. "You know, I've been going on and on, and I haven't even told you what I do here. I'm responsible for personnel and marketing"

"What a surprise."

Lydia hit Bill on the arm. "I think we're going to get along just fine." She looked toward the front of the office.

"It looks like Ron is free. Let's move quickly, before we lose him."

Bill noticed that there was only one fully enclosed office, near the windows. Everything else was modular and tight.

I can't believe all this activity in this small space, he thought.

Nick Donofrio appeared out of nowhere, spun around, and miraculously ended up in the small passageway in front of them.

"Welcome," He said.

"Thanks Nick. I'm happy to be here and looking forward to becoming part of this energy."

"Sounds like one of us already, doesn't he," Lydia quipped.

Immediately, three or four people attacked Nick, asking questions, all nudging closer in this confined area. It appeared to Bill that he was listening to all the questions at once. There was no order. His face was animated as he answered simultaneously. His eyes glossed over, and he appeared to be in a state of ecstasy.

"Let's move on before we get injured from flying body parts," Lydia said. "Even though he loves it, I can see the pressure building on Nick's face. If he doesn't relieve himself soon, this could be the end."

As Lydia led the way down the hallway, Bill questioned. "Relieve himself?"

Before she could answer, a loud and deep vocal sound filled the air.

"What in the hell was that?"

"Oh, you'll get used to it. That's Nick's release valve. You may not hear it at all, or you may hear it several times in a day, depending upon his pressures."

She stopped and looked at Bill, raising her hands in an all-accepting way. "Hey, if that's what he needs to eliminate the stress, so be it."

The door was open, and as they approached the office, Ron stood up and walked around his desk, shaking Bill's hand.

"We're really glad you're here. I wasn't positive that you'd be interested in the position."

"Well, it wasn't an easy decision—for a lot of reasons. But I feel the opportunity is a good one. The traditional thrifts may be in for more troubled times, and your approach sounds exciting. Besides, both you and Nick are great salesman."

Ron smiled and looked over at Lydia.

"Thanks. Let us talk for a few minutes."

"Okay. Bill, if you need any help, I'm available," She said, as she turned and walked back into the maze.

"Have a seat and push the door shut, if you would."

Ron took a sip from his cup and looked up. "Coffee?"

"No thanks—I'm all coffeed out."

"Did Lydia have a chance to give you a little background?" Ron continued, as he sat down on the edge of his desk.

"Yes. She seems very personable."

"Not only is she personable, she's extremely competent; no preconceived ideas about banking."

Ron hesitated, looking out the window and then back at Bill. "I know this is your first day, and this may sound somewhat egotistical, but I'm going to say it anyway. With people like Lydia, this business is like taking candy from a baby—I mean, the competition is nonexistent. Their buildings are on almost every corner, but they've been out to lunch so long, they've no idea what the man and woman on the street wants or needs—but Lydia does."

"For instance?"

"She gives our people as bad a time as our customers will when they're not treated as they should be. She can be a real pain in the ass. On the other hand, the employees understand and respect her for it. They understand, because we're a real team, along with our customers.

"But that's enough praise for Lydia," He said, grinning, as he stretched in his chair. "Let me start your informal orientation by giving you some of our operating philosophy."

"I'm ready," Bill said, as he pulled a pencil and pad out of his briefcase.

"We have several customer focus groups. They tell us what they want, and it's our job to give it to them."

"Seems like a logical approach."

Ron raised his eyebrows slightly. "You notice that I didn't say quickly."

"No, I didn't—why would you not want to take care of your customers quickly?"

Ron smiled. "Well, the timing of the transaction is in the 'what they want' part of our formula. Usually younger and middle-aged customers want their service quickly. But many of the older folks want you to spend some time with them. Banking is an extremely important part of their lives at that age, and they don't necessarily want it to pass quickly. That's especially true if the customer lives alone. They want someone to talk to for a while, to show them some attention. If our lobby is where they feel comfortable doing that, that's great. We think we're lucky to be chosen. And you'll notice as you meet our branch managers, they're very likeable; not what most people would define as bankers. You know what I mean—kind of boring and somewhat stiff?"

"Sure."

"Naturally, we also have some customers who want to transact business quickly. It's also our job to satisfy them."

"Well, based on your performance thus far, that philosophy appears to be working," Bill said.

"We're betting our futures on it," Ron said, as he stared into his coffee cup for a few seconds, and then looked up.

"You know, Bill, I may have jumped way ahead on you. I think it's important to go back to the beginning. You'll need a sense of history in order to know and understand who some of the players are."

"Whatever you say. Naturally, I'd like to know as much about the company as possible," Bill said, leaning forward slightly.

"The idea for this organization actually started with a main-line Philadelphia law firm, Latham Parish, and three of its' partners. They felt the time was right to start a new financial institution, and everyone told them that they were crazy.

"The industry was losing a ton of money, and they were certainly contrarians. On the other hand, they believed that a new company wouldn't have to operate the traditional way."

"Borrowing short and lending long, resulting in tremendous risk," Bill interjected.

"That's right. Then they decided that the company should be located in Florida."

"Because of the vast savings-base of the retiree community?"

"Well, that's partially the reason. They also located here because they wanted to be able to keep their suntans most of the year, with clients who could generate almost unlimited fees."

"Well, there is something to be said for year 'round suntans," Bill quipped.

"Sure," Ron said, smiling. "Anyway, now they have the tan they wanted, and the firm collects the revenues it expected. Fees for organizing the company, fees for legal advice, and fees for closing loans. A small money machine that they hope will develop into a big money machine in Florida; the number one savings deposit state in the country."

"Sounds good so far. So, how many of those people have been placed on the board so that Latham Parish can maintain control?"

"There are a few, but they give the impression that independence is paramount. On the other hand, a number of the non-firm people have also been handpicked."

"So, at minimum, there has to be some loyalty there," Bill said.

"Sure," Ron responded. "I wouldn't say that the firm pulls all their strings, but they certainly lean in the firm or firm member's direction when necessary. It can be frustrating, but that's part of the job."

"I understand. I've seen it time and time again. For some law firms, there's a fine line between giving legal advice and trying to control a client's destiny—especially when that destiny is tied in closely with legal fees."

Ron shook his head. "That's why I wanted you with us, Bill. You haven't even met the people from Latham Parish, and you know what they're all about."

"That's business, unfortunately. So, who are the directors?"

"I'd like to review those folks with you at a senior staff meeting—additional input from your peers would be helpful. Besides, I don't want you getting information overload today."

"That's fine," Bill said, smiling. "I am probably trying to take in more than I can digest."

Ron looked at his watch. "Listen, I've got a meeting outside the office in a few minutes, so I have to go. Lydia can give you more background and get you temporarily situated."

"Great," Bill said, getting up.

Ron stood and put his hand on Bill's shoulder. "I want to

tell you again how happy I am that you decided to join us. I know it's going to work out very well for us, and for you. You won't be sorry you left Palm."

"I haven't given it a second thought," He said, lying.

"Is that you, Stephen?" Andrew asked, as he heard the front door close.

"It's me," his partner responded with little enthusiasm. He walked into the living room, sitting next to Andrew on the couch.

"So, First State's not interested?"

"You got it," Stephen responded, staring at the floor.

"Fuckers."

"I really think that they made up their mind weeks ago, but just kept us hanging."

"So who's left?"

"Well, we still have a half dozen or so."

"What are our chances?"

"I think they're still good, but each rejection is a little humbling—you know what I mean?" He looked over at Andrew.

"Yeah," He said. "Loud and clear."

Lydia looked up and smiled as Bill approached her desk.

"Are you ready for me again?"

"Yes, ma'am," Bill said, sitting down in her guest chair, bumping his leg against a partition.

"I'm really sorry for the tight quarters; we're planning to move within the next year. In the meantime, we'll have to make due with scattered inefficient space and short-term leases. Actually, your joining us now is great. We can really use your help with the whole process."

"That's what Ron and Nick have mentioned. Do you have any specific location in mind?"

"Nothing definite yet; probably somewhere in or around Boca."

Lydia hesitated, then reached across the edge of her desk and put her hand on Bill's shoulder.

"Listen, I really hope you're not discouraged with all the uncertainly and craziness you've seen and heard."

"Well, I'd be lying to you if I told you I had no concerns, but so far, today has given me some reasons to feel that I made the right decision. I love the energy and direction."

Lydia smiled. "You won't regret coming with us."

"Good. Now that we've got that straight, tell me more about Dawn," Bill said.

"You may be sorry. That's my favorite subject."

"You may be the one that's sorry. I ask a lot of questions."

"We'll test each other then," Lydia said, as she sat up and took a deep breath. "First of all, one of Ron's greatest skills is marketing. With his knowledge and my chutzpah, we can't lose."

"Say more."

"Okay—we segment the market. Then we give each group what they want, instead of one generic offering. Since retirees are such a big part of our business, that group is a perfect example. I don't know if you know this, but the people who have typically settled on the east coast of Florida are Jews from the Northeast—New York, New Jersey, Connecticut, etc.

"On the west coast, it's Christians from the Midwest— Indiana, Iowa, Ohio, and Michigan. Naturally, it's not universal, but pretty much the case.

"Before I continue, however, I'm going to throw in a disclaimer," she continued with a comical pseudo-serious tone. "We have no prejudice against any religion or people. In fact, just the opposite is true. We love everyone.

"Our board is split almost down the middle: half Christian and half Jew, so we try to be extremely objective."

She nodded her head. "Now, I'll continue. We don't know why Florida has settled the way it has, nor do we care. But it's a fact, and we use that information to our marketing advantage."

"For instance?"

"Well, at our grand openings, we open at dawn—a little play on our name."

"Got it."

Once Lydia started talking about Dawn, Bill noticed that she seemed to rise to a new level of excitement. Her expressions and hand and arm movements flowed together perfectly.

"We buy all the seats for a showing at a local movie theater, and the first two hundred people in line at the opening get free tickets."

Bill sat up in his chair and looked at Lydia with a questioning expression on his face. "In line for what?"

Lydia looked back at him. Her smile broadened, and she said impishly, "For our branch to open."

"I don't believe it. People stand in line when it's still dark to open an account in a banking institution."

She leaned forward. "Mr. Casey," She said enthusiastically, "this in not just any financial institution, this is Dawn Savings! And this is not just a branch opening, it's a celebration!"

She sat back, appearing to be very satisfied with her explanation.

"Okay, okay, okay. I'm not used to this kind of thing. Continue on, Ms. Lewis."

"On the east coast, we give away tickets for *Fiddler on the Roof*, and we serve bagels and cream cheese.

"On the west coast, it's *Annie*, and we have donuts—and then, we add little touches along the way."

"Are you successful?"

"Are we successful? Wait until you see our opening in Miami Beach next quarter."

"I'm looking forward to it," Bill said.

CHAPTER 3

Stephen Carr and Andrew Larson were sitting on beach chairs with their eyes fixed on the white-capped waves. It was evening, and they were nursing bottles of Corona; nothing had been said by either man for the last quarter of an hour.

"I don't think we're going to make it," Stephen finally commented, still staring forward.

Andrew said nothing.

"We've been turned down by too many financial institutions in South Florida—I think the word's getting around."

He looked over at Andrew. "Maybe we're being blackballed—the bankers seem to be a relatively tight club here."

Taking his eyes off the water, Andrew looked at his friend. "We'll make it," He said, raising his voice, intensity building in his face. "But it won't be easy. We'll continue to have a lot of opposition. On the other hand, once we get our break, we can't let anyone push us around."

He took a deep breath, looking back at the water, and then turned toward Stephen again. "Success is our destiny—there's no question about it."

Stephen smiled and looked back at the ocean. "I hope you're right—we're down to the short hairs."

Andrew grinned, but remained silent.

"So, who's taking minutes today?" Ron asked, looking around at his management team.

"I'm up," Nick responded, opening his loose-leaf binder.

"Well, the numbers look very good for the quarter, both in asset growth and earnings," Ron said. "If we keep this up, I'm sure we'll be one of the top performers in the country this year in our asset class.

Any comments or questions?" Ron asked, as he slowly paced around a financial flip chart that he and Bill were using to update the senior staff.

"When is the offering scheduled?" Nick asked.

"Bill?" Ron responded, passing on the question.

"Within the next month or so," Bill said. "Ron will start his road show, and go to five or six locations over a two to three week period with our lead investment banker, Marshall Morgan.

"I'm getting some very positive feelings from our market makers, so I don't think we're going to have too much trouble."

"Great," Nick responded.

"As a second item for me," Ron continued. "I'd like to discuss a few of our board members for Bill's benefit. Even though he's met them, I want to give him some background. And naturally, please chime in, if appropriate."

Nick and Lydia both nodded.

Ron looked at Bill. "We have sixteen people on the board. Some sleep at the meetings—generally those are the Latham Parish people. They typically only wake up to vote. But there are a few movers and shakers.

"First of all, there's me, and I act as both the president and chairman."

"That's one for our side," Nick commented.

"Then we have Ed Marks, Alan Adamson, Arnie Cohen, Neal Sparkman, and Lad Lingrum. Ed is a former lobbyist—

he still has quite a few connections in Washington that we may want to tap in the future. Alan Adamson is a retired salesman from Grand Rapids, Michigan. He's a young retiree—in his late fifties—and kind of a feisty individual. He's dependable, very dependable."

"If you ask Alan to do something, it gets done," Lydia added.

"Let's see," Ron said, hesitating slightly, "then there's Arnie Cohen. He's one of the nicest people on the board. He comes from a relatively wealthy family in upper New York State—textile business. He never really had to work very hard, but appreciates people that do. The last two, Neal Sparkman and Lad Lingrum, were both born and raised in Palm Beach County. Neal's a pharmacist and Lad's in the haberdashery business. Lad's a little narrow of thought—if you're not a happily married white Christian, he tends to look down on you."

"He's being very nice," Nick said. "Lad can be a real asshole."

"But he knows a lot of people in town," Ron continued, "and his connections have helped our business. Neal's somewhat caustic, but both seem to be well intentioned. Generally, we have a very good board."

Ron looked at Lydia and Nick. "Does that do it, team—as far as the major players anyway?"

"That's it," Lydia said.

"Good short review," Nick added.

"Great," Ron said, acknowledging Lydia, and then looking over at Nick. I want you to update the group on the lending area, but first, why don't you touch on what I've asked you to do in the Alpha Division?"

"Alpha Division?" Lydia questioned, raising her eyebrows.

"Right—we didn't know what else to call it," Nick responded, grinning. "I know we all feel that Dawn is a new beginning in the financial institution industry. Well, we never want to lose that creativity and experimentation that got us this far, so Ron has asked me to head up a new division with that philosophy in mind."

"Exactly what is its' mission?" Bill asked.

Nick paused, appearing to collect his thoughts, then continued. "Its' mission is to continually generate and implement ideas that will allow us to successfully venture down new avenues, benefiting our customers, stockholders, employees, and the organization, in general."

"The real watershed in this whole effort will be group contribution," Ron added. "That is, we need ideas from all the people in this room, from the rest of our staff, from our customers, from our stockholders, etc. Nick and the others we add to that division will refine, massage, and test whatever they can, to assist Dawn's overall thrust. It's very much of a cooperative effort."

"Sounds great," Lydia commented.

"I think it will be, but we have to recognize that everything we do won't be successful—and that's okay," Ron continued.

"Research and development have proven to be invaluable components in the manufacturing industry's long-term durability. It's relatively unheard of in this business, but we're going to give it a shot."

"I'll have more for you over the next several weeks," Nick added. "Most of my time, however, will still be spent in lending.

"As we all know, since Bill's here to handle the finance, accounting, and operations areas, I've been able to concentrate more in the acquisition, development, and construction segment of our business. The one to four family residential lending, with subsequent sale in the secondary markets, did us well, but we can't possibly grow as quickly or profit as much as we'd like with such a narrow focus. These ADC loans, as they're generally known, give us much more of an opportunity to reach some of our more aggressive financial goals."

"So what are you thinking?" Lydia asked.

"Well, we've been working right along with a few small speculative builders. They've been successful, and therefore, so have we. But they're minor ADC borrowers, strictly tied to residential.

"We've been looking at increasing our commercial development lending that supports all the new housing that's being built west of town, where most of the expansion is taking place."

"Nick, can you give us a few examples."

"Sure, Lydia. In all rapidly developing areas, the infrastructure lags—schools, churches, sewage systems, office parks and shopping opportunities, for example. So our thought is to focus on one or two of those areas and become specialists."

"Isn't the risk in that type of loan substantially greater?" Bill asked.

"Well, it is if the borrower doesn't have much equity in the deal," Nick said.

"And typically they don't," Bill said.

"Generally, that's true. They borrow most or all of the land purchase, development, and construction costs. But, if we expect to grow, we have to take our lending to another level.

"The key to success in this arena is in knowing your customers and having the proper underwriting infrastructure. That's why we have to create the right systems, both operational and informational. The lending division has established that goal as our main focus. Naturally, we're also developing appropriate lending relationships."

"So how's our progress in that area?" Lydia asked.

"Ron and I have been talking with Stephen Carr and Andrew Larson, two partners who have completed a few larger strip centers, running anywhere from 200,000 to 300,000 square feet in size. We looked at their work, and it's nicely done."

"Then why are they coming to us? What about their current lenders?" Bill asked.

"They're success has actually caused them to move away from the banks and thrifts they had been doing business with-they're too small. On the other hand, Carr and Larson are too small for the big banks."

"So, their success with smaller properties has pushed them into the middle market, and now they can't get financing," Bill added.

"Exactly," Nick answered. "Carr and Larson were missing a lot of opportunities because their larger competitors had the financial backing and were able to close on choice locations.

"We've been hesitant to take this type of deal to the loan committee for two reasons. The first is that we've only completed a few smaller commercial deals and they've all been tied to home building. And, secondly, Carr and Larson's lifestyles are unorthodox enough to turn off any typically conservative financial institution."

"Would you define 'unorthodox lifestyles' for me, please?" Lydia asked, with raised eyebrows.

"Yes, they're a gay couple." Nick said, matter-of-factly.

"The staid banking community down here has problems with that—and that may include our loan committee."

Ron looked around at his senior staff members. "I believe you're a good cross section of people, with different beliefs. Let me have your opinions, as a kind of preview of what we may hear from the loan committee. I know how Nick feels because the two of us have been involved in the discussions, but what are your thoughts?" He looked at Bill and Lydia.

"You really think you're going to have a challenge?" Lydia asked. "I mean, as long as it works financially, what difference does it make?"

"Well, first of all, the loan committee members are nice guys, but I'm not sure I'd consider them liberals, especially Lad Lingrum. The fact that it may be profitable for Dawn may not be a significant enough consideration. Secondly, Carr and Larson have had some success with their shopping center niche, but they don't have any money to put into the transactions. They've evidently spent everything they've made. That could be a problem with the loan committee. If a situation turns sour for one reason or another, they walk and we're stuck with the property."

"If I was on the committee, that's where I'd have some trouble," Bill said.

"But they have no history of foreclosures or even problems," Nick said.

"That's true," Ron added. "That's why I'm willing to fight for this relationship.

Nick, summarize the first deal they proposed for Bill and Lydia."

"We have an application going to the loan committee for an ADC loan on a 350,000 square foot shopping center near the corner of Military Trail and Atlantic. It's a great location, and financially it looks very good for them and us."

Ron sat back up in his chair. "So we'll see if we get any flack. What else, Nick?"

"I'm trying to develop a correspondent relationship with a banker in Miami—Dr. Angel Oro. We haven't defined the structure yet, but I think we can do some business together. I'll bring you up to date as soon as I spend a little more time with him."

◆

Bill walked past Sylvia Clavetti, Ron's administrative assistant, comically tipping his nonexistent hat and continued into Rob's office.

"So what did you need me for chief?"

"Well, I wanted to spend a few minutes discussing an invitation we received from the Philadelphia Analysts Association."

Before Bill could respond, Sylvia spoke from the outer office, her voice somewhat stressful.

"I really believe you need to..." Sylvia said, raising her voice.

"Excuse me! Ron, I must talk to you," Stephen Carr said irritably, as he sashayed past Sylvia and into Ron's office.

"I told him you were in a meeting, Ron," Sylvia said, appearing exasperated.

"That's okay," he said calmly. "Bill, this is Stephen Carr— hopefully, one of our future loan customers."

Bill looked at Stephen. He was tall—six-foot-five—and muscular. His tan was deep, and with his blond, curly hair, he could have been a model. His handshake was gentle for a man of his size.

"Bill is our chief financial officer, and responsible for much of our internal administration."

"It's my pleasure, Bill," Stephen responded. He immediately looked at Ron.

"I'm curious as to why you used the word *hopefully*, when you introduced me."

"Well, you're not a customer yet, Stephen."

"Why is that? Does my sexual preference have anything to do with the loan committee's delay?" Stephen asked, in an almost defiant manner. "I know your board and Lad Lingrum. It's certainly not an easy sell."

"Have a seat."

"I don't want to sit."

Ron took a deep breath. "Stephen, this is a big deal for us. We're really in the infancy stage, from the standpoint of commercial real estate lending, and the committee needs adequate time to study the request. Once this loan is approved, and I believe it will be, any future requests should move through smoothly. Nick is trying to standardize your shopping center deals, so the committee format will be like a cookie cutter in the future."

"The red tape is your internal problem," Stephen said. All I know is that if we don't get our approval soon, I'm going to a lender that understands how important timing is to developers." He started to walk out the door.

"There's no financial institution in this area that will respond faster," Ron said. "I know that and you know that. You're a new customer, and we're doing what we have to do to move the approval process along."

Stephen stopped and turned.

Ron walked over to him and put his hand on Stephen's shoulder. "We know how critical timing is to developers, and we're interested in building a long-term relationship with you and Andrew."

"So, when will we know?" Stephen asked. His tone was almost friendly now.

"We have a loan committee meeting next Tuesday that I've called just to concentrate on your deal and relationship. You and Andrew are very important to us—don't forget that."

"Okay, fine. I've got to go."

Ron walked Stephen out to the front door.

"That guy can be such a shithead," Ron said, as he shook his head and walked back into the office.

"I am truly impressed with the way you handled him," Bill said. "He walked in your office angry, and left appearing as though he felt someone cared about him."

Ron smiled. "Well, the potential in this segment of the business is phenomenal. With our rate, points, and equity kickers, we'll make a mint. Plus, I think he has a good product."

"What kind of kicker would we get on a shopping center loan?"

"An out-parcel in the center. We'll try to get one of the prime pieces. Then, if the area has the demographics we're interested in, we'll put a savings or lending office on the property that we paid nothing for. If the location doesn't suit our purposes, we'll sell it to one of our competitors."

"I know we've talked about mistakes before," Bill said, "but what about busts with this type of lending? The developers we'll be dealing with are not going to have any substantial cash equity in their deals. If they're wrong, they'll walk away from the projects. Then it's our center, residential development, warehouse, etc., and our problem."

"Not to worry. Nick and I decided to set up a loss reserve of one percent for all ADC loans for those mistakes.

That's the typical percentage for commercial banks on non-secured loans. It should be plenty for our deals, since we have the property as collateral, as well as personal guarantees."

Nick walked into the office late on Sunday morning. He heard singing in a nearby cubicle and walked over to see who was playing the radio.

"Bill."

"Hey, Nick, how are you? And what are you doing in today-it's Sunday?"

"I'm fine. I'm here because I forgot some things for a loan origination office visit early tomorrow. More importantly, how are you?"

"Great!"

"That's funny, you don't look so great—and I say that to you as a friend," He said, with a smile.

Bill laughed. "Well, friend, I've got a lot to do."

Nick's smile disappeared, and he scratched his head. "I know. I'm afraid I wasn't as organized as I should have been. I apologize for that."

"No big deal," Bill said. "I'll get it done, and then I'm sure it'll be smooth sailing."

"Maybe so, but in the meantime, six or seven late days per week without a break will kill you. I've done my share of putting in too many hours, but lately I've been trying to mix work with some relaxation."

"So what do you suggest, Dr. Donofrio?"

"Your prescription is a long weekend on the beach—you, Marie, Lillian, and I."

"I'd love to, but I really don't have the time..."

"Listen," Nick cut in, "it'll be here when you get back."

Bill took a deep breath, looked around his desk, and then back up at Nick. "Where on the beach?"

"I knew you'd come around," He said, twisting to sit on the edge of Bill's desk. "As executive vice-president of lending, I can introduce you to Ocean Sands, a beautiful development located about an hour and a half north of here. We financed all the end loans on the project."

"And there are units there to rent?"

"No, not for us. Dawn owns a gorgeous unit—right on the beach. It's part of that additional consideration we always talk about. Anyway, it's available for the board and senior management team. Lillian and I have it on Labor Day weekend, and there's plenty of room for both couples. How about it?" He asked, almost pleading.

He's right, Bill thought. *This place is going to drive me nuts unless I start to pace myself.*

"I'll talk to Marie. We really haven't spent much time together lately, and a weekend away would be nice."

"I did the same thing when I first started at Dawn, and there are times I fall back in the rut, but, like I said, right now, I'm maintaining as healthy a balance as possible in this crazy place. I work my ass of during the week, but on the weekend, I try to get away."

"Okay," Bill said, playfully shoving Nick's shoulder. "Now, leave me alone so I can get out of here at a decent hour."

Lillian Donofrio welcomed the Caseys as they entered Dawn's condo unit. Bill put down the luggage.

Nick was standing near the kitchenette. "Before you do another thing, how about a drink to start the weekend off right?"

"Terrific," Bill enthusiastically answered. "How about a gin and tonic?"

"Me too," Marie jumped in.

"And I'll have the same," Lillian added.

"This group is easy."

"Nick used to be a bartender," Lillian said.

He stuck his head out from the kitchenette. "A long time ago—in college. I had a lot of fun."

He finished mixing the drinks and helped Bill take his luggage to the bedroom. Then they all grabbed their glasses and walked out on the screened-in porch, overlooking the ocean.

"Isn't this beautiful?" Nick asked.

"Gorgeous," Marie answered. "It was really nice of you two to ask us to come out here with you."

"Well, it's yours to use as much as it is ours. There's no question that we work hard at Dawn, but some of the benefits are great," Nick said.

Lillian grabbed her drink and held it up. "I'd like to make a toast to a new friendship—hopefully, one that will last a long time."

They all clinked their glasses together.

Bill looked at Marie and smiled.

They spent much of Saturday walking the beach, collecting shells, watching the seagulls dive for their dinner, and listening to the ocean persistently attack the dry sand, and then retreat.

The sun was hot, but a steady breeze was blowing off the ocean. Nick was lying on his stomach on a beach towel, partially propped up on his elbows and reading. Periodically, he took a drink of his gin and tonic.

Bill was next to him, lying on his back with a sand pillow under his head. His eyes were closed, and he looked inanimate, except for a thin plastic hose that would move slightly as he sucked his screwdriver from a jug sitting on a small beach chair next to him.

Bill squeezed the top of the hose, temporarily stopping the flow.

"You know, Nick, my grandfather came from Shanagarry, a little town in the County of Cork, southeast Ireland. When he came here, he had nothing. He worked hard, probably died as a relatively young man because of it, but he never complained. He had a modest, but nice house and a beautiful family. Because of what he didn't have in Ireland, he treasured things that we take for granted. After a few drinks and a good meal my grandmother prepared for all of us, he'd get himself a toothpick, push back a little in his chair, and say to me, 'Billy, this is the life.'

"It's amazing what the immigrants went through," Bill continued. "And for that matter, still go through in this country. Most of us don't have the problem of providing basic necessities, and yet we feel that our lives are so difficult."

"It's all in the priorities," Nick responded, "the individual value system."

Both men were quiet for several minutes, letting nature have the floor and willingly becoming part of a much larger composition of sand, water and sky.

"Hey, Nick."

"Yeah, Bill."

"Even though I've been with Dawn for six months now, I really don't know a lot about some of the people there. I guess, I've been shoulder deep in work and haven't taken the time to ask many questions, unless they were work-related."

"So, who do you want to know about?"

"Ron."

"Sure."

"Give me the full personal tour. I mean, I know from the 10K I read before I started that he has an MBA from Harvard, and he told me he was raised in Connecticut. What about his wife, Sara? I understand she's also a professional."

"Yeah. She's an engineer, and she's done some development work up in New England. She took time off from her career for a few years when their twin boys were born, but now she's back at almost a full-time pace."

"Where's she from?"

"Rhode Island, I think. Her father is a pharmacist; kind of an interesting guy. I met him last year when he came down to visit. Have you read about the Professional Exchange Program the government started several years ago?"

"Not really. Is he involved in some way?"

"Yeah. The U.S. sends representatives from various professions to foreign countries, and visa-versa. The compensation isn't much, but I guess the participants do it for the experience. It must be interesting. He's been in several exchanges."

"And his wife?"

"She goes too. She was in education, but they decided to do this thing together. She taught French—now she learns the language wherever they go."

"They do sound like interesting people. What about the twins? How old are they?"

"I think they're five or six. They have a live-in nanny to coordinate the household. Been with them since the kids were babies."

Bill took a deep breath and closed his eyes, enjoying the feeling of the sun on his body. He was listening to the relaxing sounds of the seashore, and started to take another drink. He hit air, and blindly moved his hand along the side of the chair, checking the screwdriver container. His hand brushed up against a leg. He was startled, and looking up, noticed that the hose had been pulled out of the jug. Shading out the sun with his hand, he recognized Marie's silhouette.

"Okay, boys, time for dinner.

'Bill, I hope I didn't destroy your life support system."

"I think I'll survive," He said getting up. "Where we going?"

"Lillian and I thought we'd just go to the restaurant here in the development," Nick said. "It's easy and it's good."

"Sounds great," Bill said.

The sliding glass doors were open, and the humidity was unseasonably low. The breeze was wonderful. Darkness had settled in, but the sound of the ocean was a beautiful reminder to the diners that the Atlantic was only a short distance away.

"Great recommendation," Bill said, finishing his coffee.

"That chef is fantastic," Marie added.

"I knew you'd like it," Nick said, getting up.

Bill looked around, searching for the waiter. "What about the check?"

"Oh, don't worry about it," Nick said, putting his hand on Bill's shoulder. "This is part of our business. Since we financed this project, we don't pay." He walked ahead and escorted Lillian out the door.

Bill hesitated, but their waiter was nowhere to be seen.

Marie looked at Bill and shrugged her shoulders. "You heard the man."

"Yeah, I guess."

❧

The sweat was pouring off both men as they cooled down on Sunday morning, lying back on shaded benches next to the tennis courts.

"It looks like the improvement in the humidity was short-lived," Bill said, rubbing his towel through his hair.

"You said it. But we had a great workout," Nick said, playfully punching Bill.

"Let's stop at the pro shop. I have a few things I want to get."

"Sure," Bill said.

❧

After looking around the store, Bill picked up a container of balls and walked over to the register. He pulled his wallet out of his duffel bag.

Nick was already at the checkout. He had several pair of shorts, a shirt, hat, and a container of balls. The clerk was putting his items in a bag.

Bill noticed that no cash, checks, or credit cards changed hands.

"Got what you need?" Nick asked, turning around and putting his hand on Bill's wrist once he noticed the wallet. "Don't worry about it. It's all part of the relationship."

Bill shook his head. "I can't. This is something I want for me. It's a personal purchase."

He walked around Nick and paid the cashier, who looked surprised, but accepted the money.

As they walked out of the pro shop and back to the condos, Nick looked over at Bill. "It's no big deal."

He hesitated slightly, but his companion didn't respond.

"You're talking about peanuts here."

Bill stopped. "Look, you can do what you want, but that doesn't mean I have to agree with you."

"No it doesn't. But we usually work as a team at Dawn," Nick said, his eyes piercing.

"How can you consider yourself objective as far as any future lending decisions with this borrower, if you take gifts from him?"

"So what are you saying?"

Bill took a deep breath and forced a smile.

"Look, Nick, I'm not trying to pass judgment. You've been great to Marie and me. Let's just end the conversation with an agreement between us that we look at the lender-borrower relationships differently."

"Sure," Nick responded with no emotion as he turned, continuing his walk back to the condo.

CHAPTER 4

Bill arrived at Dawn's new Miami Beach location, a storefront in the downtown business district, slightly before daybreak.

As he approached the office, he noticed several hundred white-haired retirees in line for free show tickets, trinkets, a chance to win a trip, and other prizes. It was just as Lydia had said it would be. As he walked up to the front of the building and the sun started to rise, the door opened, and the crowd moved forward as a single mass. Two off-duty policemen were standing near the entrance trying to keep order.

"Hey, you. Get out of there!" one of the policemen shouted in a definite Brooklyn accent.

"But, I know these people," responded a retiree, trying to move up a little farther in the line.

"I don't care who you know. The people ahead of you waited for their place in line and so can you."

"But..." the potential customer went on.

"No buts," the policeman responded. "Go back to where you were, or I'll take you to the back of the line."

The retiree looked irate, but Bill noticed that he did what he was told. The confrontation seemed to quiet the crowd to an almost orderly state.

Bill approached the policemen. "Hi, guys. I'm Bill Casey with Dawn. How are you doing?"

"Fine now. I'm John Jark and this is Gary Fisk," the New Yorker responded.

"Can I talk to you for a few minutes, fellas?"

"Sure," they both responded.

The trio moved just out of the earshot of the line. "I thought you were here to protect the customers," Bill commented with a smile.

The second policeman had no recognizable accent as he spoke. "We are, Bill. Protect them from each other. We take off-duty security jobs all the time, and we never have a problem with robberies or vagrants, but these retirees have actually inflicted physical injuries on each other.

"Most of these people are from New York, and they forgot they left for a friendlier place. That's why we have to be so tough on them. If you're too nice or indecisive, they'll eat you up—women or men, makes no difference."

"Bill," a voice beckoned from the front of the office. "We can use your help up here."

He could barely see Lydia waving her hand.

"Okay, I'll be right there."

"Thanks for the help, guys...and the education."

"Anytime."

As he moved inside, he noticed a table full of bagels, cream cheese, coffee, and orange juice. He grabbed a glass of the latter, and moved through the crowd smiling.

Lydia was trying to keep the line moving. "If any of you are interested in becoming our customers today—and we'd love to have you—please have a seat over there on the left," she said, motioning.

"I'll get you with one of our savings counselors as quickly as possible." She raised her index finger. "And while you're waiting, we'll bring you tickets for our drawings for some nice gifts we'll be giving away each hour today.

"Just before closing," she said more deliberately, "we'll pick our grand prize winner."

"So what's the grand prize, dear?" asked one of the early

birds, near the front of the line. "An all-expense—paid trip to Boca Raton?"

Everyone within the near area laughed, but Bill noticed that Lydia continued on without missing a beat.

"How would you like a free trip to the Bahamas for a week?" She asked.

Several ooh's and aah's made it obvious that the grand prize was a winner.

The early bird, obviously not shy, continued. "That's much better than the other banks around here give us. All we ever get from them are radios, pots, and pans."

"You'll get those here too, at our hourly drawings. The Bahamas trip is an extra, because you're special to us. We want to show you how happy we are that you're here today, and giving us the opportunity to become your bank."

"I'm not sure if you mean all that honey, but you sound good anyway."

"Where did you say I should go to open a new account?" another of the early birds asked.

"I do, and right over here. Bill, can you make sure everyone fills out one of these forms for the drawings? Then I can concentrate on coordinating the new accounts."

"I'm here to serve."

"I knew you'd say that."

"Nice breakfast table back there," he commented.

"In about an hour, our popcorn and lemonade wagon will be here."

"Popcorn and lemonade wagon?"

"Right. Free snacks—the customers love it. A retiree operates the business, and really enjoys getting out once in a while. He's invited to all kinds of activities, but I think we're the only financial institution he does."

"Well, I'm looking forward to a sample. So, when is Ron coming?"

"Probably in an hour or two, when we really get busy."

"Busier than this?"

"Wait until about noon. It'll be unbelievable, and I love it," She said, as she moved away to help a customer.

"I can tell", Bill said.

Stephen Carr had 300 pounds of free weights above his body. He just finished his last repetition of his bench-press set and was taking a two-minute break before he started again. He heard the door open and tilted his head back to see Andrew walking toward him.

"So how's Orlando?"

"We're there," Andrew responded, as he sat down on another piece of exercise equipment facing Stephen.

"The potential is phenomenal. We can get a great buy on a parcel in an area that's about to explode—all we need is money."

Andrew hesitated, running his hand through his hair, scratching his head. "So, how'd your visit go with Jameson?"

Stephen took a deep breath, sat up, and turned toward Andrew, pursing his lips. "I really don't know. I'm probably nuts, but I believe that he's doing what he can to get the deal done.

He won't admit it, but I think he's going to have trouble with his loan committee and board—especially Lad Lingrum."

"He's the asshole you and I talked about?"

"Yeah," Stephen responded, staring into space, expressionless.

Andrew moved to the bench. "Listen. Everything's going to be all right. I can feel it."

Stephen continued to stare, saying nothing.

"Hey!" Andrew said, putting his hand on Stephen's neck. Let's go over to Nassau for the weekend—we need a break."

"We can't afford a trip now. You know that", Stephen responded.

"Sure we can. The flight is cheap, and we can stay with Otto and Terrell."

"They're in Nassau?"

"For the last year."

"I guess I haven't kept up," Stephen responded soberly.

"You've been letting this financing problem get the best of you. Listen," Andrew continued, "we're going to get this lending relationship, and we'll be in the big bucks. I'm convinced."

"You seem awfully confident lately."

"Is that good or bad?" Andrew asked, still grinning.

"It's good, as long as you realize it could be disappointing if we're turned down."

"Stephen, at this point in my life, those words are no longer in my vocabulary."

"Yes, ma'am, a trip to the Bahamas is the prize—the big prize that is. We're also giving away all those items against the wall over there in drawings every hour," Bill said, pointing. "Just fill out one of these registration slips and drop it in the big box at the end of the table."

"This better be a winner, young man," his elderly challenger stated, with a sober look, but a glint in her eye.

Bill put his arm around her shoulder and looked down into her eyes. "I can't guarantee anything, but if beauty and luck are connected in any way, you've got a great chance to take home a prize."

"I think you should make an appointment and get your eyes checked," she responded.

He squeezed her shoulder and laughed as he started to pass out slips to several other potential winners.

"No, I think I can see just fine," He said, looking back at her.

Bill noticed two young female staff members from Dawn's West Palm Beach office approaching him.

"Lydia said you might need some help," said the first.

"They have plenty of people over at new accounts," added the second.

"Sure. That's great," He said, as he looked at the crowd. "People just keep pouring in. I can't believe there are this many people in Miami Beach."

"You should see outside."

"I think that's what I'll do," Bill responded. "Do you have any questions?"

"No," the first said, smiling. "It seems like Dawn has a drawing of some type every other day, and we're always asked to be there. We're fine," She said, waving him away.

He looked outside as he walked toward the new accounts desk. *John and Gary seemed to have their crowd-control techniques firmly in place*, he thought.

"Lydia. Let's take a break. The girls can handle this."

"You're right. It's only going to get busier. We might as well get some of our strength back," Lydia said, smiling.

They walked through the congested and noisy lobby, out past the crowd at the entrance and the tempting popcorn wagon.

"This is much better," She said. She took a deep breath taking in the gorgeous Florida day and put on her sunglasses. They sat on a street bench in front of a yogurt shop.

"What's hoppin?"

Bill and Lydia looked behind them for the familiar upbeat voice.

"The commander and chief," Lydia said with a smile. They both got up and greeted Ron Jameson, bowing comically, but he continued on past them, sniffing the air as he walked by.

"Wait a minute. We didn't go over your schedule yet."

"Popcorn," He said, pointing. "That smell is driving me crazy. I'll meet you inside."

"Lad Lingrum", said a voice over the telephone.

"That's right—he lives on the island, and he's listed."

"When do you want it done?"

"This weekend."

"You're not serious—this is Thursday."

"I know what day it is, and I also know that you owe me big time."

"Fine," said the voice, emphatically. "Can you give me a little help on this, or is that too much to ask?"

"He and his wife go to dinner most every Saturday night at the Palm Beach Club on Peruvian. In fact, he has a reservation this week at 8:30 p.m. He's old, and he drinks too much. This should be a piece of cake for a man of your ability."

"Wait a minute," the voice said, tersely. You want me to whack them both?"

"Whatever it takes—with no witnesses."

The office was busier now than it had been all morning. Those that were early had their tickets to Fiddler on the Roof and were now opening accounts, eating popcorn, drinking lemonade, or just schmoozing outside the office.

Bill noticed Ron working his way toward them, smiling and commiserating with the customers, offering them some of his popcorn.

"So, team, what am I supposed to do?"

"The Hadassah Chorale will sing 'God Bless America.' The VFW will lead us in the Pledge of Allegiance, and then you'll need to give both groups our customary thousand—dollar donation," Lydia responded quickly. "The Miami Beach High School band will follow. Their marching and music should take fifteen or twenty minutes before you and the mayor cut the ribbon."

"Lydia, you blow my mind," Ron said. He looked at Bill. "How many other financial institutions do you know of that have marching bands, complete with baton twirlers, at their grand openings?"

"There may be others, but I don't know of any. I love it."

"See why I keep her around. She keeps things interesting."

"There's the mayor. Come on, Bill—I'll introduce you to her, and we'll get this thing moving," Lydia said, as she started toward the front door, grinning.

&

Lad Lingrum stumbled out of the club on Peruvian in Palm Beach. The plush greenery surrounding the buildings on the street was beautiful during the daylight hours, but at night, it made the less traveled street even more secluded.

"Are you okay, Lad?"

"I'm fine Martha. That doorjamb gets in my way once in a while," he responded, continuing toward his car.

"Hi, folks."

The Lingrums both looked toward a voice—an

interruption in their conversation. The man approaching them was well dressed, with a suit and tie. He was clean-cut and smiling.

"I'm from out of town and slightly lost. I'm looking for the Brazilian Court Hotel."

"You're only a few blocks off, son," Lad responded.

He extended his arm, pointing in the direction of the hotel, but neither Lad nor Martha had the opportunity to say another word.

The silencer was quiet and the shots were quick. The complete encounter took less than sixty seconds. One quarter hour later, the executioner was returning the rental car. Within an hour, his flight had taken off from Palm Beach National Airport.

"So what's up?" Bill asked as he walked into Ron's living room on Sunday afternoon. Lydia and Nick were already there.

"Have a seat," Ron said, somberly. "Lad and Martha Lingrum were found murdered this morning."

"Where?" Lydia asked, shaking her head in disbelief.

"Behind some bushes, near his club. Clean bullet holes through their heads. No witnesses. No fingerprints. Evidently, someone surprised them. No apparent struggle. I'm sure the police will be around asking a lot of questions."

"Do the police think it was a robbery?" Nick asked.

"Both the Lingrums had money on them, so it doesn't appear so," Ron said. Lad knew a lot of people in town, and we all know that not everyone liked him."

Bill and Marie walked into the Hyatt in West Palm Beach for brunch.

"Honey, you go ahead and get seated. I have to check my voice mail," Bill said, walking toward the bank of telephones near the restrooms.

"This is Sunday."

"I know, but I'm working on a couple of financings and..."

"It's okay," She said, holding her hand up and continuing toward the hostess. "Just don't take too long."

Only one of the three telephones was being used. Bill dialed the number for his voice mail, listened to his one message, noting the details and hung up. As he was finishing a note to himself, he thought he heard the name Lingrum mentioned by the other man on the telephone. That individual had his back to Bill and he spoke softly, so he wasn't sure. He hesitated.

"No. I don't think they have any fucking idea. Great work."

There was some hesitation and the caller glanced over his shoulder.

Their eyes met briefly and Bill busied himself with his notebook and the caller turned back to his telephone, squaring his back even more.

"He was an asshole," the caller said quietly, "and she got in the way. I'm not concerned."

Bill put his notebook in his pocket, turned, and walked back toward the restaurant. He saw Marie in a booth, and as he approached her, he noticed Stephen Carr at a table.

"Hi, Stephen. Bill Casey from Dawn," He said, extending his hand. "I met you in Ron Jameson's office a few weeks ago."

"Sure. I remember. It's good to see you," He said, dryly. His eyes shifted behind Bill, and he stood up. "I'd like you to meet my partner, Andrew Larson."

As Bill turned, he realized that his and Andrew's eyes had met the second time in the last five minutes.

"Andrew, this is Bill Casey, the CFO from Dawn Savings."

Andrew's response came slowly as his squinted eyes focused on Bill. "My pleasure," He said. "Stephen mentioned he met you at Dawn when he was visiting with Ron. I certainly hope we can conclude this extensive analysis you guys are putting us through and start to do some business."

"Everything I've heard from Ron has been positive," Bill said. "He's working with the loan committee to get it done."

"I hope so."

"It was good to see you again, Stephen, and to meet you, Andrew."

"Yeah," Stephen responded, while his partner nodded.

Bill walked to the booth, sat down, and immediately looked at the menu.

"You look like you just saw a ghost," Marie said. "Who were those guys?"

"Two developers that applied for some financing at Dawn for a shopping center project," He said, glancing up.

"You don't like them?" She asked.

Bill took a deep breath and forced a smile. "I really don't know them well. I only met the big guy a few weeks ago for the first time, and the other one, just now."

Marie reached across the table and grabbed Bill's arm.

"Look at me. You sure you're okay?"

"Sure. I'm just hungry."

❧

"Ron," Sylvia said over the intercom, "Detective Callahan from the Palm Beach police is here to see you."

"That's fine. Send him in."

Ron walked to his office door, welcoming a very erect and official-looking plain-clothes man.

"Mr. Jameson?"

"Ron, is fine, Detective Callahan."

"Tom."

"Okay. Fair enough. Please, have a seat," Ron said, gesturing toward the couch.

"I'm taking for granted that you're here concerning the death of the Lingrums."

"That's right. I know Mr. Lingrum was on the board here—in fact, I've talked to a few of your local directors. Can you tell me if you know any reason why anyone would want to kill the Lingrums?"

"Well, based upon what I read in the paper and heard on the news, their jewelry was untouched, and he had money in his pocket. Evidently, it wasn't a robbery."

"It doesn't appear so. It really looks more like an execution."

"Well, Palm Beach was Lad's home. He was born here, so he knew a lot of people. He was also a successful businessman and could be tough at times. I'm sure with his personality, he created some enemies. But honestly, I have no idea who would want to kill Lad or Martha."

"Based on the discussions I've had with people around town, I think Mrs. Lingrum just got in the way. No one said an unkind word about her, but you're right, Mr. Lingrum wasn't liked by everyone."

Detective Callahan stood up. "If you can think of anything to help us in our investigation, even if it seems remote, please call me," He said, handing Ron his card.

"I sure will. Lad was an excellent board member," Ron said, as he escorted the detective to the door.

The telephone rang and Stephen Carr picked up the receiver. "C & L Development."

"Stephen?"

"Yeah. Nick?"

"All done. Your loan's been approved."

"You're serious?"

"Sure. Both Ron and I told you it would happen. All you had to do was be patient."

Stephen hesitated. "I guess I wasn't very good at that—I pretty much gave up on Dawn."

"Well, you judged us too early, but that's history. And this is just the beginning."

"Nick, I know you did a great deal to move this along—Andrew and I really appreciate your effort."

"Well, I did what I thought was right. Congratulations to both of you."

"Thanks," Stephen said, as he hung up the telephone. He stood there for a minute. *This is the opportunity we've been waiting for*, he thought.

"I knew we could do it!" he yelled, running to find Andrew.

"I still can't believe it happened," Ron said.

"But the funeral's over, and the police are following through," Nick said.

"There's really not much more we can do."

"Any leads?" Bill asked.

"No, none, whatsoever. At least that's what the detective told me. Evidently, it was a professional job."

Ron hesitated. "Listen, group, I know it's difficult not to dwell on the deaths, but Nick's probably right. We have to let the police do what they do best, and we probably need to do the same."

"But it does put a damper on the excitement of moving to our new offices," Lydia said, scratching her head and forcing a smile.

"Hey, everything looks beautiful," Bill commented, as he glanced around the room trying to change the mood.

Windows stretched along the two outside walls. Ron's desk and three side chairs were located closest to the entry door, while a couch, love seat, coffee table and four well-cushioned side chairs were placed in a circular format at the far end.

"So let's see the sauna?" Lydia said, following Bill's lead.

Ron grinned, got up from his desk, and walked over to another door in the back corner.

"I know we talked about removing it, but I thought it would be a waste to pull it out. I'm not sure how much use it'll get, but what the hell."

Bill and Lydia got up to look. Bill glanced back at Nick.

"I already saw it—nice," Nick said, nodding with approval.

Ron opened the door. "Since the rest of you didn't realize I thought about keeping the sauna, you probably didn't focus on it, but here it is," he said, motioning with his hand. "We really didn't change anything-just spruced it up a bit.

"There's a small dressing area with a bench, locker, and

shower. The room in the back is the sauna itself. By the way, it's a community fringe benefit. You're all welcome to use it before or after work."

He sat down on one of the side chairs in the circle. "Enough of the tour," he continued.

"The Miami Beach opening went really well...at least from my perspective. How do you feel about it, Lydia?"

"Well, as usual, I thought the opening was fantastic."

"So what's new?" Nick quipped.

"It was terrific," she retorted. "Ask Bill. That was his first branch opening, and I'm sure he'll be objective."

"So, what about it, Bill? Was it really that great?" Nick asked.

"Yes, it was. I've never been to an opening like it, and one million dollars of savings in the first day—that must be a record."

"Not really," Ron said, laughing. "If Lydia doesn't have a million dollar day when she opens, she considers it a failure."

"That's right," Lydia agreed, nodding.

"Anything else?"

"That's it for me today," Lydia said.

"Bill?"

"I've got a couple tentative dates for you and me to speak to the South Florida Broker and Analyst Association. We can spike those down over the next week or so, and since we haven't done this together before, we should set up a time to discuss the presentation format."

"Okay. Arrange a time and date with Sylvia.

What else?" Ron asked, looking around at the team.

"Jack Graham, one of the brokers we've been dealing with north of here, brought us a potential opportunity in western Vero Beach," Nick announced.

Lydia raised her eyebrows.

"What kind of opportunity?" Ron asked.

"Well, it's a country club, partially finished."

"I like Jack, but it doesn't sound like something we'd be interested in," Ron continued.

"Normally, I would agree," Nick said. "But this is a little different. Three Japanese nationals are developing the property. The managing agent is a gentleman named Hideo Takani. I visited with him for a short time last week. Evidently, the partnership has been working on this project for the last two years, in one way or another. They probably have two to three million of their own money invested. Unfortunately, everything's moving along more slowly than expected and they've had quite a few change orders. Hideo can't finish the project with the construction money they have left."

"Who are they working with now, and why do they want out?" Bill asked.

Nick nodded. "Their current relationship is with Florida State Bank and Trust, and they just don't want to put any more money in the construction or make the permanent loan."

"So, why is this a good opportunity for us?" Ron asked.

Nick moved forward in his chair. "We love golf in this country, agreed?" He looked around at the group.

"Agreed," everyone said, almost as one.

"Well, the Japanese also love the game, and naturally, they have tremendous restrictions because of their limited land mass. So, they make their golf courses smaller, and Jack Nickalus even designed a ball for them that doesn't go as far, so they can maintain courses with similar stroke requirements.

And, do you know how many Japanese visit this country every year?"

"A ton," Lydia interjected, quickly.

"That's right. So, Mr. Takani will market in his country and over here. He'll sponsor both a Japanese and an American touring pro to represent the club. He's also trying to contract with one of the wealthier country clubs in Japan to make this its' sister organization. So for a small fee, they can play here and be treated like members. All he needs is time to finish the development, and Florida State Bank's not interested."

"Why don't you set up a meeting out there with the two of us and Mr. Takani sometime near the middle of next month," Ron said, glancing at his calendar.

"You won't be sorry."

Ron and Nick drove up to a doublewide trailer, on what appeared to be a nearly completed golf course. They got out of the car and walked over to the construction headquarters. The pleasant aroma of orange blossoms was in the air from the nearby groves. Before they could knock, the door opened, and a smiling, slightly overweight, Oriental gentleman carefully walked down the stairs.

"Mr. Donofrio," He said, extending his hand. "I'm so glad you agreed to meet with me again today."

"Mr. Takani, it's my pleasure. In fact, you're so important to us, that I brought the President of Dawn Savings, Mr. Ron Jameson."

"I'm elated that you see the potential in Old Cyprus, Mr. Jameson," Hideo said, bowing. "We can take a tour, if that would be appropriate," he continued, extending his arm in an inviting way toward two golf carts.

"I would like to see the project and to understand why you think the club would prosper out here in the middle of orange groves," Ron said. "We know that Vero is moving west, but this is quite a distance from the city's center."

"Yes it is, Mr. Jameson..."

"Just call me Ron. Do you mind if I call you Hideo?"

"No, I don't mind," he replied, smiling.

"Let's look at the course first, and then I'll tell you why I believe this project has all the attributes for success, except one."

"Would that one be patient money?" Ron asked.

"That is correct."

"We'll talk about that later," Nick interjected. "Let's go." He walked toward one of the carts.

As they drove, Ron noticed that the course was completely laid out and appropriately cleared, but there were still some drainage tiles lying along several of the fairways.

For a Florida course, the terrain was hilly, evidencing substantial fill dirt and grading work.

They stopped on what would be the tee of number seven, a one-hundred-eighty-yard, par three, most of which was over water. The elevation of the tee was built up at least sixty feet over the green. Hideo stopped the cart and waited until Nick pulled up alongside.

"It looks like it's going to be a beauty," Nick said.

"I'm extremely proud of the course. The layout was a joint effort between Stewart Bell in this country and Yasuo Kitamura from Japan," Hideo said.

"Bell is certainly well known in the United States. And I've read a great deal about golf in Japan, and what your country has done to adapt to a much more confined land mass.

Hideo nodded.

"And Kitamura is quoted often. He must be quite an authority," Ron continued.

"He likes to work in difficult situations. In Japan, it's available yardage per course. In Florida, it's making a boring flat terrain into a challenging golf course, and that's where Mr. Bell comes into the picture."

"I noticed his work as we were riding. The real trick for a designer or architect is to lay out a course that's interesting, but at the same time, not too difficult for the average golfer. You certainly don't want to scare away the vast majority of your potential members."

"I don't know if Nick mentioned my interest in golf, but I love the game."

"Yes, he did mention that you were an avid golfer," Hideo said. "That's why I thought you may be interested in my project. And you're exactly right as far as Mr. Bell is concerned—that's his specialty. He's extremely creative.

"I want to take you by the golf villas next, and then show you the site for the proposed clubhouse."

They stopped at a partially completed building near the center of the golf course. Ron noticed that there were no tradesman on the site, and it was evident that construction had stopped. The Spanish roofing tiles had been laid and the windows and doors were in, so damage from the elements would be avoided. The design of the building was attractive, and tied in well to the country club atmosphere.

They walked through two of the ten units. The rooms were painted, but the ceramic tile, carpet, and appliances weren't installed, and the finishing work hadn't been completed.

They walked out of the building, toward the carts.

"If you look through the trees on your right, you can see another building, just like this one, near number ten."

"And how far along are you there?" Nick asked.

"The same as here, but as you can see, we're at a standstill."

"So, how do the numbers look?" Ron asked.

Hideo looked at the two men and nodded. "Let's go back to the trailer and go over them."

"I apologize for the surroundings, gentlemen," Hideo said, as the four men sat around a large table in the trailer.

"A construction trailer is a construction trailer is a construction trailer," Nick said. "They're not meant to be featured in *Architectural Digest*."

"That's right. We try to keep our administrative costs to a minimum."

"Talking about money, Hideo, how much do you need?" Ron asked.

"Fourteen million," he answered, without hesitating, as he passed out the projects financial projections.

"Fourteen million!" Ron responded, wincing slightly. "How does that break down?"

"If you'll follow me on the financials I just gave you, we owe Florida State Bank and Trust nine million on the acquisition and construction loan. It's almost fully drawn, and as you could see, we haven't completed the course yet."

"So, how much do you estimate for completion?" Ron asked.

"Well, 1 million for the course, the completion of the villas and a single-family model. One and one-half million for an interest reserve, and two and one-half million for the clubhouse, including the pool and tennis courts."

"Do you really need the clubhouse at this point? I've seen new clubs operate out of a trailer or a temporary building during their infancy." Ron said.

Hideo eyes were intense. Old Cyprus did not appear to be just another real estate project to him.

"We could, but we cannot lose sight of what we're trying to sell—the complete country club image. A golf course alone won't do it.

"When potential buyers visit us, we want them to realize that they could be part of what they see and experience. Artist's renditions and models for a clubhouse just won't do it. That's especially true for overseas buyers."

"Evidently, Florida State Bank and Trust didn't agree with that philosophy," Nick said.

"No, they didn't, and that's why we've had very few pre-sales," Hideo said.

He hesitated, then rose and walked over to the window.

"Gentlemen, please join me. You must see what I see."

Ron and Nick walked over and stood on either side of their host. It was a beautiful Florida day. The few clouds that were in the sky were so perfect that they appeared artificial. Even though the young grass didn't yet cover the ground completely and the surrounding foliage was not mature, the scene was already impressive.

"Considering the upscale nature of this property," Hideo continued, "we'll need promotional weekends with food and beverage services, and overnight accommodations, if necessary. I don't want playing this course to be just an ordinary day of golf. It must be a memorable experience for all, no matter what the ability level."

Hideo slowly looked to his right at Ron, who remained focused on the picture before him.

"If you had the money today," Ron asked, "when could you finish the club?"

Hideo's response was quick.

"Since the drawings are done, and we've got the appropriate building permits, we could be complete in nine months."

"These sales projections look pretty aggressive, especially considering where you're located, almost an hour from downtown Vero," Nick said.

Hideo looked to his left. "They may be slightly aggressive, but there's nothing better within an hour's drive of Vero, and we're attempting to add even more value to a membership."

"For example?" Nick continued his questioning.

"We're negotiating an agreement with the Ocean Beach Club that would allow their members the opportunity to play golf and use our facilities. They, in turn, would allow our members beach and other club privileges at their location."

Ron looked at his watch and then at Hideo.

"We're going to have to get back to Boca, but we'd like to take these projections with us. Nick and his people will review them and probably call you with questions or to get more information."

"When can you give me your decision? I want to get the project moving along again as quickly as possible."

"I would think we would know something in about two weeks." Ron looked at Nick. "What do you think?"

"Considering what we've got in process for the loan committee, I would say two weeks is reasonable."

Hideo looked at each of the two people standing before him and smiled.

"I appreciate your consideration, and I look forward to hearing from you."

CHAPTER 5

Ron was drinking his glass of orange juice as the team wandered in at 7:00 a.m. for their Tuesday morning senior staff meeting. They took their seats on the couch and side chairs. Ron looked up.

"Nick and I had a relatively productive meeting with Hideo Takani last week."

Nick smiled.

"Why don't you update us on the other lending relationships?" Ron asked.

Nick sat up. "I'm still working on Dr. Oro, and the correspondent banking relationship we've discussed.

Carr and Larson have been with us several months now and they're rolling—three shopping centers in process, in various stages of completion. We met with Smith & Joeffrey last week."

"The syndicators?" Bill asked.

"Right. Carr and Larson plan to pre-lease, complete the project, sell to Smith & Joeffrey, and distribute the proceeds, which naturally includes our loan payoff. Then, we'll keep the cash machine going with new centers."

"Sounds good to me," Ron said.

"Anything else in the hopper, Nick?"

"Sure. Our Texas operation is doing extremely well. With the offices we've opened in Austin, Houston, and Dallas, our coverage is fantastic in another State that's growing like crazy."

"What else?"

"That's it for me."

"How about you, Bill?"

"This has nothing to do with my responsibilities, but I want to get a concern I have out on the table."

"Fine," Ron responded.

"I think that there may be a connection between Carr and Larson and the Lingrums' deaths."

Nick looked shocked. "You're not serious?"

"I am. They had everything to gain by Lad not being on the loan committee."

"And you think they would kill for a loan approval?" Nick continued, his voice growing significantly louder and his face turning crimson.

"Yeah. I overheard a telephone conversation that Andrew was having, and it didn't sound good."

"Are you sure of what you heard?" Ron asked.

"No. Otherwise I would have contacted the police."

Nick twisted around in the Queen Anne chair. "You're arriving at a conclusion with no facts—only what you think you may have heard."

"I realize that, but I feel very uneasy about the whole relationship."

"The police have been on this for months, and they have evidently found nothing, but you think you've cracked this case," Nick said, critically.

"I didn't say that there was definitely a connection. I said that I think there may be."

"Well, you're wrong, and I'm insulted that you are questioning the character of two people I've worked very hard to cultivate for Dawn," Nick responded.

"I'm sorry you feel that way."

"Fuck you."

"That's enough, Nick!" Ron interjected, raising his voice. "He's giving you his true feelings, and that's what we all should be doing with one another if we really want a strong team."

Nick continued to glare at Bill.

"What the hell's wrong with you—he's doing his job," Ron continued. "One of the reasons I hired him is because *you* guaranteed me that he was an independent thinker."

"Fine," Nick said, curtly.

"Bill, if you have anything concrete, talk to the police. On the other hand, unless Larson and Carr are found guilty of something, we can't treat them any differently."

"Whatever you say," Bill responded, with no emotion.

Lydia, how are we doing on the branch side?" Ron asked, in an obvious attempt to change the direction of the discussion.

"Good," Lydia said, timidly. "We'll be opening two more savings offices over the next six months, one in St. Pete and one in Boynton Beach.

Even with our rapid growth, the average savings balance in each office is still over $100 million."

"That's a great number for expense efficiency," Ron said.

"Nick, how are we doing with our systems and other infrastructure in the lending area?"

"We're not moving as quickly as I'd like, but we've had some progress," He said, appearing to force a response.

"If you need any help from our systems people, let me know?" Bill offered.

"We don't need any help!" Nick almost barked. "Your people don't know what they're doing when it comes to loans.

We'll take care of our own area."

"Nick, finance has some pretty good folks—think about it," Ron interjected.

Bill sat quietly, staring at Donofrio.

"We know our product," Nick answered. "Bill's people don't—we'll do just fine."

Bill and Marie Casey drove south on Interstate 95, getting off at the first Ft. Lauderdale exit.

"Do you have the directions there, honey?" Bill asked.

"Go east, young man. Once we get close to Route 1, we have to make a few turns, but I'll let you know when we get to that point."

"Okay, navigator."

"So, I'll finally have the opportunity to meet Lydia tonight?" Marie asked.

"She should be there."

"I feel like I should be jealous. You talk about her quite a bit, you know."

Bill shrugged his shoulders. "I guess I didn't realize that. She's just a nice person, who's good at what she does."

"Is there a Mr. Lewis?

"You know, I really never talked to her about her personal life, but I understand she's divorced. Ron said that she and her former husband were married for a number of years, but that he ran off with some young thing."

Bill glanced over at Marie. Her expression was stoic.

"Listen, I told you, she's a nice person. You're really going to like her."

"I didn't say anything," Marie said, smiling. "I'm looking forward to meeting her."

They continued toward the water, making a few turns, and arriving at the guardhouse entrance of what appeared to be a relatively secluded development of large single-family homes.

"I'm here for the Carr and Larson party," Bill said to the guard.

"And your name, sir?"

"Casey. Bill Casey."

The guard quickly scanned the list.

"Okay, Mr. Casey. Drive straight ahead to Dolphin Drive and make a right. You can't miss it. You'll see several parking attendants out there."

"Thanks," Bill said, as he drove away.

"My God! Look at these homes, honey. They're unbelievable. I bet they're five to six thousand square feet."

"Oh, at least, and each one is unique. Look at that beautiful old Florida style with the big porch and shutters."

"They're just beautiful. What do you think they run?"

"Well, we have the loan on Stephen and Andrew's home. They haven't been in here that long. If I can remember, it was appraised at two and a half million. Considering the size of the lots and the location on the Intercoastal, that's probably a bargain."

"Unbelievable," She said quietly, as she continued to look around the neighborhood.

The traffic started to back up and Bill slowed down. Ahead and to the right, a half dozen men and women were riding Arabian horses with full tack and cowboy clothing, including chaps, spurs, and ten gallon hats.

"So, all this is part of the country & western theme?" Marie asked.

"I guess that when Stephen and Andrew have a party, they really focus on the atmosphere. They were supposed to set up a tent on the lot next door, and" He said, glancing past Marie, "there it is."

"It's huge. How many people do they have coming?"

"I understand somewhere around four to five hundred. Nick mentioned that they expect to spend around two hundred and fifty thousand dollars."

"Our house didn't cost that much."

"Well, I understand that they're good at what they do, they make a lot of money, and they're evidently not afraid to spend it."

Bill stopped on the end of a cul-de-sac.

There appeared to be half-dozen attendants, parking cars and running back from the lot. One of the young boys handed Bill a numbered token, and quickly drove off in the navy blue Mercedes.

As they walked up to the tent, a photographer took their picture against the Southwest background—colorful horse blankets, bales of hay, and saddles. After the picture, they continued to walk through the circus-size tent to an area that enclosed three bars, two appetizer buffet lines, dinner tables, a portable dance floor, a platform with musical instruments and a portable sound system. The Old West motif was everywhere.

As the evening progressed, beautifully presented entrees replaced the appetizers in the buffet lines. Dawn employees, along with other business and personal acquaintances of Stephen and Andrew, continued to come and go throughout the evening. The band started to congregate near the platform halfway through the evening, and soon Ms. Sissie Parker, country & western superstar, moved through the crowd with bodyguards and attendants to her spot at the microphone. The tent was full and ready for action.

Bill and Marie looked around the crowd.

"This is certainly an eclectic group," he said.

"Well, Sissie certainly has her own unique style that seems to cover a pretty broad spectrum," Marie responded.

"I agree. She combines the best of country, storytelling and rock and roll."

Bill felt a hand on his shoulder, and he turned to see Lydia in a western outfit, including hat and boots.

"We were just talking about you on the way to the party."

Bill turned back toward Marie, put his arm around her, and made the introduction.

"Bill's told me so much about you," Marie said, slightly nudging him.

"Well, I can't tell you how happy I am that Bill's on the staff. It's a great company and a fantastic business, but Dawn is a little different, and we need somebody that's focused and got both feet on the ground in the CFO's position," Lydia said.

"But what about Nick?" Marie asked.

Lydia raised her eyebrows and smiled. "Don't get me wrong. Nick and I get along fine, but he's a character, and definitely off in dozens of directions. Like I said, I'm glad your husband is with us."

"He gets up every morning excited about work, so I guess he likes being there," Marie said, looking up at Bill.

"Hey, how about this party?" Lydia said. "Isn't this something?"

"All I see are dollar signs," Bill said with a smile.

"That's your problem. You financial guys are all alike," Lydia continued.

"Yeah. Smell the roses," Marie added.

"I'm trying, but I think I have a lot of financial congestion."

Sissie continued for an hour before her first break, and the audience loved her. The band reassembled for the second set, and she stepped up to the microphone.

"Ladies and gentlemen, can I have your attention?" The noise from the crowd almost immediately ceased. "Several years ago, I was fortunate to have recorded a song by Art Johnson called, 'You're My Lover and My Best Friend.'"

The crowd exploded into applause.

"Thank you. Thank you. Tonight I want to dedicate that song to my two new friends, Mr. Stephen Carr and Mr. Andrew Larson, your hosts this evening. Where are you guys?" She said, as she looked around the crowd, using her hand for an eyeshade to see past the bright portable stage lights.

Stephen and Andrew stood up near the front of the tent. They blew kisses at her and waved to the crowd. In turn, the audience applauded its' hosts. As Sissie started singing, they held hands, took a few seconds to look into each other's eyes, and then turned back to watch her.

Lydia leaned over, whispering to Marie, but loud enough for Bill to hear. "I told you Dawn was different."

Sissie finished her final encore at ten o'clock, and within fifteen minutes, the crowd started to thin.

"So, what do you want to do?" Bill asked.

"How about a nightcap?" Marie answered.

"Sounds good to me," Lydia said.

"Hey, gang, how'd you like the party and the show?" Nick Donofrio asked as he walked up behind the group.

"It was fantastic!" Marie answered quickly.

The others nodded.

"What does your agenda look like for the next hour or so?" Nick asked.

"We were just trying to decide where to go for a nightcap," Lydia said. "Any suggestions?"

"Sure. Why don't you come next door to Stephen and Andrew's place? Sissie Parker is over there with some of the band members. You're invited, if you'd like to stop over," Nick said. He turned and walked toward the house.

"We wouldn't want to disappoint Sissie, would we ladies?" Bill asked.

"Not on your life," Marie said, shaking her head.

They walked through the double doors into the expansive foyer. The marble floors were covered with oriental rugs and several pieces of eclectic artwork, mostly modern.

A perfectly symmetrical circular staircase with exquisitely formed railings acted as the main focal point to the second level, and to the property overall, with several hallways on the first floor emanating from its core. A lavish crystal chandelier centered the staircase and hung between the first and second floor.

Marie pulled Bill close and whispered in his ear, "Were these fellas well-off before Dawn started to deal with them, or is this newfound success?"

Bill leaned down and said quietly, "Let's talk on the way home."

Stephen walked from the back of the house with Nick, meeting them near the front door.

"How about a quick tour?"

"We'd love to," Bill quickly responded, as he continued to look around the foyer.

"We've got quite a few guests that I need to spend some time with, but Nick has volunteered to show you around. Okay?"

"Let's go," Lydia answered.

Each room was more beautiful than the next. The

bedrooms had sitting rooms and fireplaces, and the bathrooms were large and mirrored, with oversized Jacuzzi tubs in each. Artwork, both paintings and sculptures, was everywhere.

As they were walking down the staircase, Bill asked, "Is all the artwork original, Nick?"

He looked back, answering sharply, "I doubt if they would buy anything but originals, but you'll be happy to know that we didn't lend them any money for the artwork!"

"Nick, what's the problem. I'm truly impressed. It's all very beautiful."

"Fine," he responded curtly.

"So what's next, Nick," Lydia interjected, trying to change the subject.

Nick reverted back to his previously pleasant persona and smiled. "I'm taking you back to meet some people. Follow me, please."

Bill looked at Marie and raised his eyebrows as they descended the staircase.

From the time they entered the house, they had heard music from several hidden speakers in each room. As they entered an entertainment wing, Bill realized that the music was live, being played by a group of musicians, evidently hired for the after-party. The two-story room ran the complete length of the house, along the Intercostal, and made maximum use of the view with windows and sliding glass doors out to a combination deck and dock.

Nick lead the group over to a small circle of people congregating around Sissie Parker and several of her band members. He introduced everyone, invited the contingent to have an aperitif at one of the two bars, and to mingle.

Lydia and Marie drifted out to the deck, and Bill joined them with drinks. The house had been cool from the air-conditioning, but the breeze off the Intercostal was beautiful—very pleasant.

Two yachts were anchored off the pier, and several people were completing a tour of the boats. Marie and Lydia lay back in lounge chairs.

The former looked at Bill, who was staring out into the Intercoastal. "What's wrong, Bill?"

"I don't like it?"

"Like what?"

"Who's having this party tonight?"

Without waiting for a respond, he continued, "Nick gives us a tour of the house. Nick introduces us to Sissie Parker and the band members. Who's the lender and who's the borrower?"

"That's a good question," Lydia responded. "He also seems ultra-sensitive about Stephen and Andrew, generally."

"You'd be sensitive too; if you knew you were wrong."

Marie got up and put her arm around Bill.

"You're letting this get to you. Relax—we're supposed to be having a good time. Let's go inside."

He smiled and kissed her gently on the forehead. "You're right," He said.

They walked back into the house. The musicians had just finished their break, and started to play again. Stephen and Andrew were mingling and flitting around Sissie. A few couples started to dance, and the bars and dessert table were getting busier.

"I don't believe it," Bill whispered to Marie and Lydia.

"What?"

"Andrew Larson is dancing with a woman...and not just dancing. This blows my mind; he's actually necking with her. All this time I thought he was gay. He must be AC, DC."

"Maybe she's a he," Marie whispered back.

Bill shrugged his shoulders.

"Well, you could be right," Lydia answered. "Look, here's Nick. He knows all these people. Let's ask him.

Nick," she called, "we need you to clear something up for us."

"Sure," He said, walking over to the group. "What can I help you with?" He was back in his jovial mood.

The trio congregated closely around Nick.

"We noticed that Andrew was dancing with a young lady, an attractive young lady at that," Lydia said, softly.

"And?"

"Well, we're all aware of Andrew's sexual orientation... or, at least we thought we were."

Lydia was fumbling over her words.

"Is she a he, or is Andrew just, ah...flexible?"

Nick turned, putting his hand on Lydia's shoulder, but looking at Marie and Bill.

"You're right, she is a she — and as you mentioned, Lydia, a quite attractive she — at least from my perspective. But, I believe you mentioned Andrew's flexibility — she is also his sister, who's visiting."

With that comment, Nick left, and walked back toward Sissie and her current contingent.

"If I had not seen it with my own eyes, I would never have believed it," Marie said. "A brother and sister," she continued, shaking her head.

"Real close family," Bill said, grinning.

The Caseys were driving north on Interstate 95.

"I didn't mean to cut you off earlier when you were upset about Nick," Marie said, "but there's nothing you could do about it tonight."

"Oh, I'm not mad, honey, and I agree—tonight wasn't the time or the place," Bill responded."

"So what do you think?"

"What do I think? I think I'm feeling uncomfortable. And I'm not only concerned about the Larson/Carr relationship. Nick just doesn't appear to have any integrity. I don't have anything concrete, but I think there's more going on here than meets the eye."

"So, what are you going to do?"

"Watch him close. Maybe talk to Ron. But for the time being, leave it go and give him the benefit of the doubt. I may be jumping the gun."

"Probably," She said, hesitantly.

CHAPTER 6

"Yes, sir, are you checking in?" the parking attendant asked as Ron got out of his car at the World on the Bay Hotel & Club in Coconut Grove.

"No, we'll just be here for a few hours," Ron responded. He took the ticket he was handed.

"Where do we meet them, Nick?"

"We're supposed to let the front desk person know that we're here, and he'll get them. They're evidently meeting with the owner."

They walked out to the far end of the sidewalk, looked up at the building, and then out at Sailboat Bay.

"The location is gorgeous—best part of Miami, but the building looks a little tired. It needs some work," Ron said.

"I agree. Let's see what the inside looks like."

They walked into the lobby and up to the front desk.

"Yes, gentlemen. Checking in?"

"No. I'm Ron Jameson and this is Nick Donofrio. We're here to meet Stephen Carr and Andrew Larson."

"They've been expecting you. Please have a seat, and I'll tell them you're here."

Ron and Nick sat down. The small lobby looked much like the outside, Ron thought. There was a definite musty odor, but the staff looked good. They all had tropical open-collared shirts and tan slacks. They were polite and appeared to be service-oriented.

"Gentlemen," Stephen said, walking into the lobby and greeting Ron and Nick warmly.

Andrew followed suit and said, "We'd like you to meet the current owner of the hotel, Mr. Patricio Martinez."

An older gentleman, with gray hair and matching well-trimmed mustache, walked forward and smiled.

"This is Ron Jameson, the president of Dawn Savings, and Nick Donofrio, the chief lending officer."

"I've heard some very nice things about both of you from Stephen and Andrew. It's my pleasure."

"And ours," Nick responded.

"Why don't we go up to my office where we can be more comfortable? Then I'll take you on a tour of the hotel."

"That's terrific."

Their host led them down the hall.

They entered the elevator, and Patricio pressed the button for the seventh floor.

"So how's your occupancy been?" Ron asked.

"Not as good as I'd like, but let me explain.

When this property was built, this was it on Sailboat Bay, except for a few mom-and-pop operations. Now, we have several gorgeous hotels within a mile or two, a couple within walking distance."

"So, the competition's strong," Nick remarked.

"Yes it is," Patricio acknowledged.

"When I bought the hotel five years ago, I considered the hotels that were already here and visualized what I understood was scheduled to be built; that's how I came up with the idea of 'theme' rooms-I wanted to create something different."

"Stephen mentioned the concept, but I'm sure we'll get a clearer idea of what you've done during the tour," Nick said.

Patricio nodded as they got off the elevator and walked to an end suite.

"This is my office and my home, gentlemen. I welcome you. There are soft drinks and coffee on the table. Please help yourself."

The drapes and sliding glass doors were open, and Ron walked to the balcony, almost in a trance.

"What a view. No wonder they call it Sailboat Bay. There are hundreds of them out there."

"Every day, I get down on my knees and thank God for giving me the opportunity to live here as long as I have," Patricio said. "But it must end soon. Come sit down, and I'll explain why I've put the hotel up for sale."

After helping themselves to beverages, they settled down around the dining room table.

Ron looked at Patricio. *He appeared to be a little worn, like his hotel,* he thought. *Patricio probably put everything he had, monetarily, physically, and psychologically, into the property. Maybe he has finally realized that he just can't continue.*

"Gentlemen, as I said, I bought this property five years ago. I was a relatively wealthy man, and I put several million dollars of my own money into the transaction. The hotel was appraised at twenty million, I paid fifteen million and my bank gave me a loan for thirteen. Some of my money went into the theme renovation we talked about earlier, and an interest reserve, so I could get on my feet with the operation.

"I wanted this hotel to be different. A place people would want to return to, not only because of its location, but because there was so much variation.

"For locals, in addition to special weekend getaways, I opened a private club in the restaurant, with parties and other activities. Actually, that part of the operation has done extremely well, but its success has taken a great deal of work. We've tried very hard to make this a special place."

He looked down at the table and massaged his eyes with his hand.

Except for his voice, there was complete silence.

"Unfortunately, before I came, the hotel had a terrible reputation as a drug haven. The previous owner catered to the Latinos here, as I do, but he had several bad apples, as you say. It took me a long time to eliminate that stigma. Now, we're on an upward trend, but as I said, the new hotels are tough competition. My bank wants me to sell. They feel that more time and money are needed. Neither they nor I have the time, nor want to spend the money."

"So, how much do you owe?" Nick asked.

"I had an interest-only loan during this first five-year period, and I ran out of my reserve a year ago. I've paid a little out of the operation, but not much. So thirteen million, plus approximately one year's interest."

"And how much do you want for the property?" Ron asked.

"Sixteen million—fourteen and a half or so for the bank and a little for me. I realize I could wait out a higher price, but I have to get out.

"I'm getting old before my time. With some of my personal funds I didn't put into the hotel and the money I'll get from the transaction, I'll retire from this part of my life."

He was quiet for a few seconds.

"How about a tour, gentlemen," He said. Patricio stood up and smiled, appearing to regain some energy.

"Sounds good to me," Ron said.

"How about you fellas?"

"We're ready," Stephen responded.

"Now, I can't show you all the rooms—I don't think our guests would appreciate the intrusion," He said as they walked down the hall. "But I'll show you a few of the standard rooms, a few suites, and finally one of the two penthouses. One is leased out as a residence, but we keep the other one open for guests of the hotel."

They took the elevator to the eighth floor and entered the suite directly above his. Again, the view of the bay was outstanding.

"This," He said proudly, "is the Egyptian room."

"I feel like I'm in a Sheik's tent in the desert," Andrew said. "We didn't see this room the last time we were here. This is fantastic."

"It was occupied when you were here last. It is nice. As you can see, the netting over the king-size bed, the palms, the muted desert colors, the camel blankets, and even the wooden mummy coffin we use as a base under the glass table, add to the atmosphere. We try to get into our guests' imaginations and include things in each room that they may think about in relation to a specific location."

Over the next twenty minutes, they visited the Nigerian, Mexican, French, and German rooms. The penthouse was a three-bedroom suite, stretching across half of the building, with a balcony running both east and south. The Jacuzzi was placed at the southeast corner of the master bedroom, giving the occupants a view of the bay.

"Shall we go down to the restaurant for some refreshments?"

"Great," Ron answered.

"Can we pass through the kitchen?" Nick asked.

"Sure."

They took the elevator down to the second floor.

"Well, here we are. As you can see, the staff is getting ready for our lunch service.

"We don't make any money at mid-day to speak of.

There's not much drinking, unless we have a party of some sort, and as you can imagine, that's where the margin is. At dinner, we do fairly well."

Ron noticed that the kitchen was spotless, and the help again appeared happy to be there. Patricio took the group into the meat locker and the liquor cage, explaining some of the controls in place to reduce pilferage. They walked through the double swinging doors into the restaurant and lounge. The light that filled the room was almost all natural, emanating from the numerous large windows.

"On a clear night, with all these windows, it can be very romantic."

"I bet," Nick commented.

They had coffee and talked about the Coconut Grove revitalization that was taking place.

When they were finished, Patricio stood up. "Now, I'll show you another jewel in the somewhat tarnished crown of the World on the Bay. Follow me."

"I love this," Andrew said, looking around at Ron and Nick.

They walked out of the restaurant into an outdoor canvas-covered bar. The breeze was pleasant, and down below, they saw the pool and the surrounding area. The scene looked like it came from a tropical island, with large palms and bamboo plants everywhere.

"Let's go down and have a closer look."

There were several young ladies and men taking advantage of the sun. The glistening deeply tanned women in bikinis looked like they were models advertising some exotic resort.

"I feel like I'm on the beach in Rio," Nick said.

"They certainly add to the value of the property," Ron said, looking at Patricio and nodding at the hotel guests.

"I bet you brought them here today just for our tour."

"I didn't, but that's not a bad idea," Patricio responded, laughing.

He moved ahead of the group. "Let me show you something else we're proud of."

He walked past the pool and up a walkway that was edged with large bamboo and palm trees, hibiscus bushes, and lush ground cover. The area was completely cut off from the pool by a beautiful green blanket of foliage with red accents. The others followed him to an opening. An oversized Jacuzzi appeared to be set in a tropical paradise. Its' lip was covered with stone, making the odd-shaped tub look like a lagoon.

Ron stopped. "This is exceptional. You really captured the island paradise here and should be proud, Patricio."

"I knew you'd like it, and I decided that the best way to end our meeting should be in a place of real beauty, and here we are. Do any of you have any questions?"

"How about the last few years' financial statements and performance reports?" Nick asked.

"We have those. We'll make copies and send them over," Stephen responded.

"I don't think we need anything more today, do we, Nick?" Ron asked.

"No, but I'm sure while we're driving back we'll think of something. You know how that is."

"I know," Patricio said. "It happens to me all the time. If you think of anything, just call me, and I'll send what you need overnight."

"Great," Ron said.

"Talking about driving back, guys, Andrew has an errand to run down here. Can I catch a ride with you?" Stephen asked.

"Sure."

"Patricio," Ron said, as they started to walk past the pool, through the gate, and out to the front of the hotel, "we are impressed with your hotel, but even more so with you, and we appreciate your time."

"My pleasure."

They pulled into traffic, heading north.

"So you're serious about this hotel, Stephen?"

He turned and looked at Ron. "I've never been so serious about anything in my life."

"But that's not your business."

Stephen shook his finger at Ron. "Listen, Ron, you've told me that you always wanted Dawn to have an entrepreneurial twist."

"I do."

"So, it's good enough for you and Dawn, but not for Andrew and I."

"But we're a lender. That's what we do."

"But you do and will do much more than that—you've told me so"

"I think he's got you, Ron," Nick said from the back seat.

"Besides, we won't run the hotel. We'll have a professional manager."

"Like Patricio?"

"Maybe someone like Patricio for a year or two."

"And then what?"

"Well, do you think Andrew and I would get involved in the highly competitive Coconut Grove hotel business unless there was an unusual opportunity—something with tremendous potential?"

Ron looked back briefly at Nick. "I'm afraid to ask this man what's up his sleeve."

Stephen turned and looked straight ahead, beaming. "This could be unbelievable."

"All right already. What do you want to do?"

"We want to convert the property into a gay resort."

Ron was silent.

"Did you hear me?"

"Ever so clearly," Ron answered quietly, continuing to stare at the road.

Stephen looked back at Nick, who raised his eyebrows, tightened his lips, and remained silent.

"Oh, I see," Stephen said, looking from Ron to Nick while he spoke. "You probably figure that you've already bent over backwards for these two fags. You've done more than anyone else would do for us, right? I mean, you're probably saying to yourself, we're liberal, but these queers are pushing us over the edge. Is that right, guys? Well, fuck you both."

Ron looked at Stephen and then away. Nick said nothing.

"Listen, you better-than-thou bigots, whether you like it or not, the gay and lesbian business is out there now, and it will only get bigger. Do you know that there are places we can go in this country and not worry about our sexual preference? And you know what? They're always busy. Even closet gays go, because the security is tight.

Again, I ask you, can you imagine the potential?"

The silence persisted.

"Damn it!" Stephen yelled. "Pull the car over."

"What?" Ron said, looking strangely at Stephen.

"You heard what I said. Pull the car over!"

Ron slowed down and turned onto the soft shoulder. "Listen, Stephen, don't get out."

"Get out. Who in the hell is getting out? We're two hours from home. The only way I could get you to listen, not just hear, but listen, was to have you stop the car.

There are tens of thousands of gay men who would be attracted to a place like World on the Bay. With some cosmetic improvements, it could be paradise. This hotel is in one of the most sought-after vacation states in the country, and in the best part of Miami, no less. We'd have constant full occupancy, and a private club that wouldn't quit."

"So, what are your reasons for wanting to wait to change the hotel and club?" Nick asked.

"Well, even though we'll have others manage the property from the hospitality industry, Andrew and I want to know as much about the gay market as possible. We'd like to visit several of the resorts that are now operating successfully, and see why.

"We've talked about this a great deal. Some of our friends have gotten into ventures that have had great potential, but since they knew nothing about the business, they made some poor decisions and failed. We don't want to do that.

"Besides, Patricio is doing a good job. If we can convince him to stay a year or so, think about how much more we could learn about the basic business. What do you think?"

"Does Patricio know what you want to do with the hotel?" Nick asked.

Stephen turned and looked at Nick. "Are you shitting me? He would die. He probably doesn't even know we're gay."

Ron raised his eyebrows and took a deep breath and thought for a second.

"I've read all about the tremendous opportunities in gay and lesbian marketing. On the other hand, I can't see our board going along with it. Can you, Nick?"

"It'd be a tough sell."

"I think you'd better be able to justify the hotel acquisition without having to fall back on the gay angle, if you expect to get the loan from Dawn. I don't believe the loan committee would go for it any other way.

"After you own the hotel, you can do what you want, when you want, as long as you make your payments and you're operating legally."

"Fine, but we need a reasonable debt service, with interest-only for the first couple of years. We'll put some money in up front to show our good faith, but we need at least your prime rate."

"That's fine, but we'll want some type of additional consideration," Nick jumped in.

"Like what?"

"Probably a percentage of your gross revenue after some threshold."

Stephen shook his head. "You guys are always trying to take advantage of the situation."

"Listen," Ron said. "Whatever we'd want would be reasonable. If we're going to take this risk, and it is significant, we must be compensated for it.

"Naturally, we'd also have the right to audit your books and records at least once per year."

"And you're so trusting."

"We have to be objective. We're a shareholder-controlled company, regulated and examined by several governmental agencies. That's not even considering the good business judgment that we should be exercising," Ron replied.

"Okay, you can get back on the interstate. We talked enough."

Ron cautiously broke back into traffic.

"Andrew and I have to think some more, and so do you, but I believe that we'll want to go ahead."

"Send those financial reports along with some projections, and we'll talk a little more next week," Ron said slowly.

❧

It was just after six o'clock and about seventy-five people were milling around the Dawn office pavilion for its' quarterly employee get-together. Beer, wine, and snacks were served, and the gathering gave the senior staff an opportunity to interact on an informal basis with all the corporate employees.

Lydia Lewis was talking with Sylvia Clavetti.

"So what's going on with you and Jack Graham?" Sylvia asked with a smile, both on her lips and in her eyes.

Lydia appeared shocked. "Well, we've had coffee a few times, but that's only because Ron was running late, and he asked me to keep Jack busy," she responded, hesitantly.

Sylvia grabbed Lydia's shoulders, facing her, and looked directly into her eyes. "You've been divorced for three years, for God's sake. You're still a young and very attractive woman."

Lydia looked down at the floor.

"When you talk about work, there's fire in your eyes," Sylvia continued, "but your personal life's a different story. It's like I'm talking to two different people. You deserve another relationship—you have so much to give," Sylvia said.

Lydia took a deep breath, looked up and forced a smile. "I know—it's just difficult. When Ralph and I were married, it was forever. I never thought it would end, and when it did, I felt so inadequate."

"Most of us make that promise for life, but this is not a perfect world. You gave it your best shot. It didn't work out, and you've had time to be depressed. You were entitled to that feeling, but by now, it should be over."

Lydia was silent and looked away.

Sylvia touched Lydia's chin, gently turning it so their eyes met again. "We've known each other a long time. You know I love you."

Lydia nodded.

"But you've got to get over your divorce and move on. I think the trite phrase, 'life's too short,' is very appropriate here." Sylvia raised her eyebrows.

"I know, I know," Lydia replied, looking away. "But he's married," responding with some force.

"Lydia, you and I both know from the Dawn grapevine that he hasn't lived at home for the last two years. He's supposed to be in an efficiency apartment near Dixie and Forest Hill."

Sylvia looked over Lydia's shoulder and noticed Jack Graham at the far end of the pavilion; at the same time, he glanced over at them and started to walk in their direction.

"Time to get lost," Sylvia said, winking.

Lydia turned and looked behind her, almost immediately smiling.

"So what are you doing here, Jack?" She asked, pulling him a little closer to prevent being overheard.

"I came here to see you."

"But this is an employee get-together. You might be asked to leave," she whispered.

"I'll take my chances," He said, his eyes fixed to hers.

"Jack, how are you tonight?" Ron Jameson asked, temporarily breaking the euphoria.

"I'm great," Jack responded, glancing tenderly at Lydia.

"I didn't realize you were having an employee function

tonight. I brought a deal in to the loan department a little late, and no one was there. Martha, at the switchboard, said everyone was out here. Should I leave?"

"No! Certainly, not. Have a bottle of beer or some wine and enjoy yourself," Ron answered, as he started on his way to a group of employees from the lending department.

"See—no problem," Jack said, turning back to Lydia.

"You were lucky. But, now that you're legal, let's go get something to drink and have a few snacks."

"Okay, I'll follow you anywhere."

Lydia led the way down the hallway toward the executive office wing.

"You shouldn't have gotten me all that wine. I'm a little tipsy," She said, giggling.

"I know you don't believe me, but there really is a sauna off Ron's office."

"Well, I'm sure it's there, but I've just never seen it."

"Then tonight will be a first," she responded, as they walked into Ron's suite.

She opened a door that looked like it was a closet and walked in, turning on the light.

"See, here's the changing area, with a bench, locker and shower." She continued back and opened another door, rustic looking. "And here's the sauna itself."

He moved forward, putting his arm over her shoulder and stretching to peer into the room.

She turned to look at him. Their faces almost touched, but they didn't pull away from one another.

"You know, Lydia, I've thought about this moment for a long time, and now I feel like I'm a little like a sixteen-year-old kid again."

"For a sixteen year old, you're pretty smooth, Mr. Graham."

Lydia looked into his eyes.

He brought her closer, kissing her gently, pulling away slightly, and then kissing her again.

Jack's hand moved from the small of her back to the top of her thigh and then slowly up to her breasts.

She didn't pull away.

He moved his hand up under the back of her sweater and unhooked her bra. He continued to gently touch her and hold her close.

Then, almost effortlessly, he picked Lydia up and carried her over to the bench. He quickly spread a few clean towels on the floor, took her by the hand, and helped her down onto the impromptu love nest. As he stood over her, undressing, his eyes never lost hers.

Lydia sensuously took off her panties and skirt.

Jack knelt down, gently kissing and caressing her. Then he brought her close.

"Oh my God!" she screamed.

"Lydia, I don't know why we waited this long," Jack groaned, continuing to kiss her passionately. "I..."

"Yes, that's right, Tim. I'll see you at nine-thirty at the Hyatt. Terrific. Bye." The voice carried through the sauna door.

Lydia and Jack froze. "That's Ron out there," she whispered.

"Do you think he heard us?"

"I don't know. I hope not, but we were kind of loud."

Suddenly, Ron rapped on the outside of the sauna door.

"I'll see you tomorrow, Lydia. Have a good time," He said, as he left the office.

Chapter 7

The telephone rang, and Bill tapped his speaker phone button, "Bill Casey, may I help you please?"

"How about taking a ride with me to the airport?" Ron asked.

"Sure," Bill responded, not knowing why, but really not caring. *I need the break*, he thought.

"I'll drive. Meet you out at the car in a few minutes."

"Great."

By the time Bill opened the door, Ron was already inside, cooling the Mercedes down. It was September, still hot and humid in Florida. Bill took off his suit coat and threw it in the back seat.

"I can't believe this heat," Bill said, as he slipped into the car.

"What did the people down here do before air-conditioning?"

"Good question," Bill answered. He looked over at Ron.

"The timing would have been right to discover deodorant."

"That's for sure."

They started driving north on Military Trail. Once they cut across to Interstate 95, the airport was only fifteen minutes away.

"So what's at the airport?"

Ron glanced at Bill. "I'm not sure. Stephen Carr called me this morning. Evidently, he and Andrew want to show us a plane they want us to finance."

"I heard they were already sharing a Lear with two or three other groups. Why would they need any more air time than that?"

"I don't know, and that's why I'm a little concerned. You know that whatever they want, it's got to be bigger than what they have—it's their way of life."

Ron and Bill pulled up to the field gate near the executive aviation terminal. An attendant walked up to the car.

"Jameson and Casey visiting Carr and Larson," Ron said.

"Yes, sir."

He stepped back into the guardhouse, and the gate on wheels rolled open. Ron drove out onto the apron, stopping behind Carr's black Porsche 911. Stephen and Andrew were standing near the aft air stairs of a 727.

"All of a sudden, my stomach's in knots."

"I knew it," Ron said, shaking his head and closing his eyes.

Stephen and Andrew approached as Ron and Bill were getting out of the car.

"Hey, thanks for coming out," Stephen said.

"Yeah. We really appreciate this," added Andrew, shaking their guests' hands enthusiastically.

That guy is so transparent, it's unbelievable, Bill thought.

"Well, we've got something exciting to show you," Stephen said. "I'll lead the way."

The four climbed the stairs into the main cabin. The inside of the aircraft was completely redone. All the standard airline seats had been removed. As they walked down the center of the aircraft, there were two video game tables, with swivel chairs to the right. Halfway through the main cabin to the left, Stephen opened a door and the entourage followed him into the master suite. A king-sized bed with a cherry headboard matched the accompanying furniture. The carpet was thick dark brown, and comfortable. The bathroom was small, but rich looking, with an antique Victorian tub and gold fixtures.

Stephen was quiet while they were in the master suite.

Once back in the main cabin, he commented, "Pretty impressive, huh?"

Andrew just smiled.

"There's no question about it," Ron answered.

Bill nodded in agreement.

"This is the airplane Andrew and I have been leasing from a Saudi sheik over the last few months."

"What about the Lear?" Ron asked.

"Oh, it's just too small for all our friends. When we get this one, we're out of that deal."

"So, why are we here?" Ron continued.

Stephen turned quickly on his heels and said, "We're not done enjoying the plane yet. Look what's ahead of the bedroom."

Stephen walked forward. "We've got our bigger than first class seats up there, and on the wall is our Air Show. There's a control panel between those seats."

Stephen was a large man, but he moved nimbly around the cabin, showing off his new toy.

"You can set your destination, and your route of travel will be indicated in white lights on the black screen. Then you can query to see how far you've progressed along that route, your air speed, land speed, estimated time to your destination—anything you want to know! The weather, for God's sake, I can even ask for a weather forecast. If I get tired of that, I pop in one of my videos and watch a full-length movie."

He pressed a button on the control panel. A door slid

open to an overhead storage area, revealing a library of movies, arranged alphabetically and by category.

Andrew was watching Stephen and beaming. "Isn't this fucking unbelievable?" He said, as he looked at Ron and Bill.

"Yes, it is," Ron commented, dryly.

Bill just nodded with a forced smile. *No way in hell, asshole*, he thought.

❧

Bill was reviewing the monthly financial reports. The board was meeting that afternoon, and he wanted to make sure that he had explanations for all fluctuations in the income statement.

Nick charged through the partially closed door and marched into the office.

"I finished reviewing the preliminary copies of the reports you gave us, and I want to know what in the hell you're trying to do?" His eyes were intense.

Bill looked at Nick calmly. "What are you asking me?"

"Our closings were unbelievable last month. Why aren't all those fees we generated recorded as income? You think we'll look too good, or what?" Nick said sarcastically.

"Our fee income is up for the month, but we can't—and we talked about this before—recognize fees in excess of the costs we had in closing the loans. All the excess has to be allocated over the average life of the loans closed."

Nick leaned over the desk. "If we receive fees, we should be able to recognize all of them now. What kind of bullshit accounting is this?"

Bill sat up in his chair and leaned forward. His eyes were locked to Nick's.

"We've discussed this before."

"Then humor me and explain again," Nick answered defiantly.

Bill inhaled deeply before he spoke, his eyes not blinking.

"Dawn's costs have always exceeded total fees, so we could recognize everything, but your volume has picked up, and that's good. You're not losing any income, it just has to be deferred and recognized later."

Nick calmed down somewhat and moved slightly away from the desk.

"I still don't like it."

"Well, unfortunately, I don't have any control over the way you feel or the way things are accounted for," Bill said, leaning back in his chair. "I know that we're recognizing all the income we're permitted, and the excess will benefit Dawn in the future.

At the board meeting, I'll explain the whole concept again, and what a great job our lending department did last month," Bill said, as he moved forward, folding his hands on his desk. "And, I'll have Len Schwartz from Carlton and Knapp visit with the lending staff and explain the theory of cost allocation and matching revenues and expenses."

"That's the least you can do," Nick said, as he turned and walked out of the office.

He's unbelievable, Bill thought, shaking his head.

"Thanks for coming, Len. I'm not sure whether they're good, bad, or indifferent, but new regulations and laws regarding accounting seem to be determining more and more of the way we operate." Bill said, as he looked out over the Atlantic from the balcony of the Miami's Fontainebleau Hotel.

"It's all part of the accountant's Full Employment Act, and the partners at Carlton & Knapp, including myself, think it's great," he responded, chuckling.

"I know you do, but on the productive side, having these periodic update meetings for our people makes a big difference in the way they think. And it was my idea."

Bill shook his head in comedic disbelief.

"Amazing," Len said, smiling.

"I can explain all day long, but bring someone in from the outside with a briefcase, and they listen."

"It's like that all over," Len responded slowly, mesmerized by the ocean.

"It is beautiful, isn't it?"

"Fantastic. The feeling of tranquility up here is indescribable."

Bill took a deep breath, gazing at the ocean, and then looked back at Len.

"We were lucky to get everyone together; it's getting to be more and more difficult, but this secondary mortgage conference was the perfect place. After the meetings are over, we're having a reception for some of the attendees, including a few people from our Texas operation. Then we're planning on going out to dinner. Would you care to join us?"

"I'd love to, but I have to get back."

Nick Donofrio came out onto the balcony and put his arm around Len.

"That was great. Thanks for coming."

"When Dawn calls, I'm here."

"That's what I like to hear.

Listen, one of our potential new customers has asked us, and our guests, to dinner at his hotel tonight. Would you care to join us?"

"I already tried, Nick. This guy is strictly business," Bill said.

"You know that's not true. I have a presentation tomorrow morning, and I really have to get back and get ready. Thanks anyway."

"Who's taking us out?" Bill asked.

"Dr. Angel Oro."

"I remember you mentioning him at the senior staff meeting. Is he a physician?"

"No. He holds a Ph.D. in theology that he earned when he was in Cuba. He was actually considering entering the seminary before Castro took over. His uncle was Batista's treasurer, and rumor has it that he took part of the treasury with him when Fidel came on the scene.

"Anyway, when they fled Cuba, he decided against becoming a religious, and now the family's in the banking business in Miami. Angel is the chairman of the board."

"Guys, I've got to go," Len said.

"Thanks again," Nick responded, patting Len on the back.

"We'll do this again in about six months. I'll call you," Bill said.

"Terrific." Len said, waving as he left.

"Anyway, as I mentioned in the meeting," Nick continued, "over and above developing lending relationships, I'm trying to do the same thing with correspondent banking."

"Sounds good. He also owns a hotel?"

"Yeah, right in downtown Miami. Anyway, I thought this would be a nice opportunity for him to meet some of our people."

"I agree."

"We'll leave right after the reception. And he did invite our guests, so if we meet any promising prospects at the reception, we'll take them along."

"Terrific."

"And you're going to bring the last group, Bill—the staff that's helping us with the reception?"

"Sure. Where are we being picked up?"

"In the front. Limo. Black. The restaurant's on the top floor."

"I can accept all that," Bill said, with a smile.

Their car pulled up in front of the Calloran Hotel, and they walked through the lobby to the elevators. As they approached, a handsome and well-dressed gentleman near the last elevator smiled and asked, "Are you with the Donofrio party?"

"That's right," Bill responded.

"I am Henry Rodriguez. Dr. Oro welcomes you to his hotel. The restaurant has been closed for your privacy, and we will do everything we can to show you how much we appreciate your friendship."

Just as he finished his greeting, the door opened. The timing was perfect. They were on the top floor in no time, and proceeded to walk off the elevator.

Bill saw the other Dawn employees and strangers, he assumed were part of the Oro contingent, engrossed in numerous conversations, while a small, five-piece combo played soft Latin music. The room had numerous floor-to-ceiling windows and several large skylights, with the stars and the moon casting an enchanting glow.

Bill encouraged the others to mingle and started to do so himself. He saw Nick getting a drink and walked up to the bar.

"Your friend is a pretty impressive guy, Nick."

"Yes, he is. I'll introduce you to him later. It looks like they want us to sit down for dinner. Did you find a spot?"

"There's one across the room—I'll see you later."

Bill walked over to a table with management personnel from Dawn's Texas loan origination offices.

"Gentlemen, is this seat open?"

"Certainly," Guy Bern, from Houston, responded.

"Even though you never come to visit us, we Texans don't mind a Florida Yankee in our midst—we're liberated." He hesitated momentarily.

Bill smiled and acknowledged everyone else at the table, so Guy went on.

"You boys certainly know how to throw a party."

Bill smiled. "First of all, I will be in Texas in the near future. It's just that sometimes there's not enough of an opportunity to do some of the things I'd really like to—like visit you guys. But I'll be there soon," He said, making a point of looking at each of the staff members.

"Secondly, this get-together is just as much of a surprise to me. I don't know who this guy is we're trying to do business with, but he doesn't fool around, does he?"

"Hell no," Gil Catchen, from Austin said. "It looks like he really wants to develop a relationship. This is almost as nice as something we'd have in Texas, isn't that right, Guy?"

"Almost," he responded, nodding his head and grinning.

"You fellas never give up, do you?" Bill quipped.

"We call 'em as we see 'em," Guy said, drolly.

Bill felt someone put a hand on his shoulder. He turned around and Nick Donofrio was looking at him.

He looks like he's in a state of ecstasy, Bill thought. *He lives for this type of action.*

"I want you to come over and meet Dr. Oro. He should know all our senior people."

"Sure, Nick, I'd love to."

As they were walking across the room, Bill noticed several couples starting to dance. *That's strange,* he thought, *I don't recognize most of the women on the dance floor.*

He moved closer to Nick as they walked, and asked quietly, "Who are these women? Friends of Oro's?"

Nick looked at Bill, shrugged his shoulders, then turned back and continued to walk across the dance floor.

They reached the other side of the room, and a gentleman stood up as they approached his table. He was relatively short, approximately five-foot-two, with a well-groomed, dark black mustache. As he stood, three other men at the table also rose. They were husky, tall and stoic looking.

Bodyguards seem a little unusual for a banker, Bill thought.

"Dr. Oro, I'd like you to meet Bill Casey, our chief financial officer.

"Bill, Dr. Oro—the chairman of one of our new correspondents."

They shook hands and Oro looked directly into Bill's eyes as he spoke. His voice was low, coming from deep in his throat.

"I look forward to working with you and Dawn. I can see by the way I've been treated thus far, that your company is a first class organization—and Nick tells me you're one of the reasons."

"Nick is too kind; but thank you for your kind words."

"Bill," Dr. Oro said slowly, "I hope that this evening is something close to that with which you're accustomed."

With the lavishness of this get-together, the security people, and the gravely voice, I feel like I'm in the Cuban version of one of the Godfather movies, Bill thought.

"This is very nice, Doctor. I also look forward to

working with you and your staff. I hope to see you later in the evening."

Bill turned and walked across the dance floor to his table. He glanced over at Guy Bern.

"You missed it," Guy blurted out, with no prompting.

"Missed what?"

"I said earlier that this soiree was almost as nice as something we have in Texas. I was wrong. It's just as nice."

"I get the feeling you want me to ask you what changed your mind?"

Guy nodded.

"Okay, what made you change your mind?"

"One of our new Latin friends came over to the table and said that he could get us *anything* that would make us feel more comfortable."

"So, how did he define *anything*?"

"I'll do this like a game show, Bill. What nationality are most of the drug czars of the world?"

"Well, several nationalities, but broadly, Latinos, I guess."

"Congratulations! You're pretty smart for a non-Texan."

"But that's not all," Gil added.

"So what else?" Bill asked, starting feel uncomfortable and slightly irritated. He and Nick had tried to 'bury the hatchet', but this conversation was starting to add salt to the wound.

"He said that we could stay here tonight instead of at the Fontainebleau, as the good doctor's guests," Guy said.

"And," Gil jumped in, "he explained that those female friends of Oro were unattached, and that they mentioned to him that they kind of liked us.

"Are we being clear, or should we go over this again a little slower? We know this is very difficult for a Yankee banker to understand."

"Fuck you."

"You seem a little testy, Bill. We're just funnin with ya," Guy added, apologetically.

"I know. It's not you," Bill said shaking his head. "I'm just not sure I agree with Nick's choice of borrowers lately."

"Well, they certainly seem to want to do business with us," Guy said.

"Maybe too much so," Bill said, raising his eyebrows.

"Listen," he continued, standing. "I'm glad you fellas are having a good time, and I love your company—I mean that sincerely—but I have to get out of here."

Bill shook everyone's hand at his table, and then left without any additional comment to his host or to Nick. He caught a cab back to the Fontainebleau and drove to his home in West Palm Beach.

CHAPTER 8

"Lydia," Ron said, "we're going to start with you today. How's our branch network look?"

"You should even ask?" she answered, grinning broadly.

She got up and walked to the corner of the room, where she picked up a flip chart and brought it over closer to the gathering.

"I wondered why that was there. And you're right, I shouldn't have asked, but you would have probably told me anyway."

"You're right," She said, flipping the top sheet over.

She took a small pencil-like piece of metal off her clipboard and pulled the top, converting it to a two-foot pointer.

"I don't believe it," Nick said, shaking his head.

"Bill showed me how to make the charts."

"That figures," Nick continued.

"The pointer was my idea. Anyway, as you can see, we've almost reached our goal in each of our savings offices of $100 million or more in balances. Only one hasn't attained that level, and it's less than six months old. The chart shows you where we were six months ago in each location and where we are today."

"The next chart," She said, flipping the page, "shows where each of the offices will be one year from now, at about sixty percent of each location's previous growth."

"Why did you reduce the growth rate?" Nick asked.

"Bill and I assumed that at some point we were going to hit a level of diminishing returns. One hundred plus million is a sizable office in any organization—even Dawn's."

"And it's just a little more conservative approach in our projections," Bill added.

"Now, I have my super-chart that takes our current savings branches, slowly ratcheting down on the growth rate, but at the same time, adding in one new savings office per quarter at an initial higher growth level."

"How far out did you go?" Ron asked.

"Five years."

"What's the number?" Nick asked.

"Three and one-half billion and thirty-eight offices," She said proudly.

"And that's all de novo. Any additional companies or savings offices we buy are icing on the cake," Bill added.

"Terrific," Ron said. "Nick, how are we doing on the Arizona bank acquisition?"

"Well, I still don't understand why we can't own thrifts and banks at the same time…"

Ron raised his hand. "That's the law, but it's a problem we no longer have to be concerned about. We stripped out the branches and sold the franchise. A great deal for us. Let's not look up a dead horse's ass, Nick."

"You're right. And since that closing, the bank acquisition is moving along much faster."

"That's what I wanted to hear. What else is happening?" Ron asked.

"Lots," Nick responded, leaning forward in his chair. "Hideo Takani is marketing Old Cyprus in Japan like there's no tomorrow.

"The course itself should be completed shortly. The clubhouse is under construction, but won't be finished for several months yet.

"I was out there yesterday, and I'm pleased with the progress."

"Any presales?" Bill asked.

"A few, but nothing to speak of yet. Hopefully, as we get farther along on the clubhouse, we'll have more interest.

"Carr and Larson have six centers in varying stages of completion. We inspected the three they have on this coast last Monday, the Orlando center last Thursday, and the two on the west coast this past Monday. The center in Orlando is just about complete, and the syndication process should begin soon."

"Speaking of syndications," Bill said, "why don't we consider starting our own company? We pay some heavy-duty fees for this service. Why not do it ourselves?"

"That very question was on the tip of my tongue," Ron said.

"Nick, have your people research the possibilities of either starting from scratch, or better yet, finding a small operating company with a good track record that we can buy."

"I'm on it."

The Caseys drove up to the valet parking stand at the West Palm Beach Yacht Club. Marie's door was opened and Bill walked around his car, passing the keys to the smiling attendant. The night was cool for South Florida, but the sky was clear and beautiful. They were walking down the pier, admiring the boats.

"I still don't understand how the parking attendant knows which car is ours," Bill said. "We only come here once every couple of months, but yet, when we get to the end of the pier after dinner, our car will be there, waiting for us."

Marie put her arm around Bill's shoulder and smiled,

"It's one of the Wonders of the World, right behind the Pyramids and the Grand Canyon."

They approached the entrance way and Stephen Carr, Andrew Larson, and a stranger were on their way out of the Club. As soon as they recognized the Caseys, Carr and Larson looked uneasy.

"Uh, hi folks, how are you?" Stephen said hesitantly.

"Yeah, hi," Andrew added.

Stephen quickly recovered and greeted Bill and Marie with a handshake and kiss. Andrew followed suit.

"Do you people know Jason Daletti?" Stephen asked.

"Your name or face is familiar, but I just don't recall why," Bill said.

"Well then, Jason Daletti, this is Bill and Marie Casey. Jason's also in the real estate business in South Florida."

Turning to Jason, he continued. "And these folks are with Dawn Savings—directly and indirectly."

The smile dropped and then reappeared on the stranger's face. "Pleased to meet you," He said.

"Have you done any business with Dawn?" Bill asked.

"Not yet, but your organization's getting to be a major force in this part of the country, so I'm hoping that changes."

"How was dinner?" Marie asked.

"Terrific," Andrew answered.

"The chef here is a real artist," Stephen said, as he, Andrew, and Jason continued on toward down the parking area.

"I hope you have a nice weekend," Stephen continued, waving.

Marie looked at her husband, who was continuing to stare at the trio as they walked to the parking lot.

"So what are you thinking about, Bill? You look like you're out in another time zone."

"I was just trying to remember why Jason Daletti is vaguely familiar," Bill said, still preoccupied.

"Any success?" Marie asked.

"Yeah," He said. "I remember reading a memo from Nick to Ron explaining that the Daletti Group was selected as the new independent inspection and appraisal firm we're using in the underwriting process for a large block of Carr and Larson loans."

"So what does that mean?" Marie asked.

"Maybe nothing," Bill responded, putting his arm around his wife, escorting her up the restaurant stairs.

"But you don't really believe that," Marie said.

"Not on your life."

Bill Casey was walking down the hall at Dawn. As he was passing the file room, he noticed Connie Newman letting Stephen Carr leave through the Dutch door at the entrance to the file room, briefcase in hand.

"Stephen, how are you?"

His head jerked quickly toward the voice.

"Oh, you surprised me, Bill. I'm fine, but I've gotta run. See you."

Bill walked up to the file room door. "Connie, how are you today?"

"I'm fine," she answered, continuing to sort her work.

"What was Mr. Carr doing in the file room?"

"Oh, he just asked if he could see some of his project files. He's always so nice to me, and he's been in here with Mr. Donofrio before, so I didn't think there would be a problem."

"Well, I wouldn't let him in again.

"Practically speaking, for control purposes, I'm not

even allowed in the file room. Only file clerks and your supervisor are permitted in here.

"Mr. Carr doesn't even work for us, and he shouldn't be in the room, or be asking for any of our files."

"Like I mentioned, Mr. Casey, he's been in here with Mr. Donofrio."

"I understand. I'll talk to Mr. Donofrio about setting up some guidelines for you." Bill said, as he continued down the hall.

❧

"I know you all felt that another meeting, especially for a full day, was not something you needed in an already tight schedule. I understand that. On the other hand, too many companies in our industry operate on a day-to-day basis—in a vacuum—never really thinking about the future, and it passes them by."

He looked at each of his senior staff members, shaking his head. "We're not going to let that happen. One of the advantages we have in this business is our competition."

"We don't have any," Nick interjected.

"I disagree—we do. They're just not very effective," Ron responded. "They still want to do what they did fifty years ago. Congress isn't going to protect the thrift industry any more. We're on our own, and we must be innovative. That's why we need to have these strategic planning sessions.

"Who's up on the agenda, Lydia?" Ron asked.

"Bill."

"Okay," Bill said. "If you use your handouts, you can follow along with me."

He reviewed the history of Dawn in asset and income growth. Then, he distributed six scenarios with various financial assumptions, but the same basic operating plan.

"Bill, please explain the insurance subsidiary you're proposing," Ron said.

"Sure. As you all know, we make a few bucks on mortgage life and disability insurance. I say a few, but in relation to other financial institutions, we're doing exceptionally well. Our mailings and follow-up calls have been giving us excellent returns and our people have done a remarkable job," He said, nodding his head.

"But I really feel we can make more money from our borrowers' insurance needs."

"I thought financial institutions were prohibited from selling insurance in Florida?" Nick questioned.

"I think it's ridiculous," he continued, "that the insurance lobby is strong enough to keep us out of the market, but I understood that they had the power in Tallahassee and there was nothing anyone could do about it."

"You're almost right," Bill answered, sitting down. "I think we can get around the law somewhat. I've spent some time with Jim Allen and his son..."

"Good people," Nick interrupted.

"Yes, they are. Anyway, as we all know, he's a stockholder, and he's been with us from the beginning. They're local people, and the old man has been a major player in this community.

"The Allens and I have been discussing Dawn's potential, and we've come up with something."

He hesitated, collecting his thoughts.

"Dawn can't earn any premiums or commissions based upon sales. So, we rent the Allens' space in our building at the fair market value, whatever that is. We hand out brochures at application time for the one-to-four family borrowers, explaining the insurance programs that we have available through the Allens' agency.

"Since many of our borrowers have just arrived from other parts of the country, they don't have an agent in this area, and our company has a distinct marketing advantage — residential, life, etc., over and above our standard mortgage life and disability."

"I'm starting to like this," Lydia said, smiling.

"I knew you would," Bill responded, winking.

"Not only will we talk to our customers at the application stage, when they really want something, but our partners will continue to follow up with mailings and telephone calls," Nick joined in.

"Right," Bill said. "Then there's the commercial borrowers; they also need all types of insurance during the construction process, and afterward. Our loan officers appropriately explain the programs we have. The Allens' are available for appointments here or at the borrowers' home or business.

"Bottom line, Dawn makes money, the Allens' generate a profit, and we'll compensate the appropriate employee making the sale, in some fashion."

"So, how do we make money other than by the rent?" Nick asked.

"Well, that's really it, but the space is leased for six months. The first term is at a conservative market rate. We review the premiums collected during that period. As they increase, so does the rent."

"Is that legal?" Lydia asked.

"Well, we could get some hassle, but we're not going to announce our modus operandi to the world, and the Allens will be here using the space several days a week. I believe our approach is pretty solid."

"Bill and I discussed this possibility, and I think we should give it a try," Ron added.

"The insurance industry will be shot down on their protectionism over the next few years. If they give us any trouble at this point, I'm sure we can tie them up legally for that long."

"I agree," Nick said.

"If it's going to be successful, we'll need a strong push from Nick's lending people," Bill added.

"No problem," Nick agreed. "It's good for all of us."

"So, what are you working on, Karl?" Andrew Larson asked over the telephone.

"The paperwork supporting the leases that Mr. Carr negotiated on the centers."

"Look—I'd rather have you concentrate on the legal work for World on the Bay."

"With all due respect, Mr. Larson, Mr. Carr said..."

"Karl, Mr. Carr and I are partners—we make our decisions together. And most recently, we decided that the World on the Bay had much more long-term potential than the centers."

Karl was silent.

"Is there a problem? Andrew asked curtly"

"No, Mr. Larson. We'll get all the legal work for the hotel put to bed first, and then we'll work on the centers."

"That's what I want to hear, Karl."

"I'd like to discuss something that's been bothering me," Bill said, looking over at Nick and Lydia. The former looked confused, and the latter was adjusting herself in her seat, preparing for a confrontation that was evidently discussed before the meeting.

"I think we...the whole Dawn staff, give Stephen Carr too much leeway."

"How so?" Nick asked, sitting up straight in his chair.

"In every way. Where he's permitted to go, what he's permitted to see, etc?"

"And you still think he's a murderer. You're a fucking judge and jury, aren't you," Nick said, tersely.

"We're treating this guy like our partner."

"He is our partner!" Nick yelled, almost jumping out of his seat.

"No, you're wrong; he's our borrower—big difference."

"You know," Nick said sarcastically, "you look for trouble. I tried to let your last crazy accusation pass, but now you're pushing it."

Bill was quiet.

"He can never leave things alone," Nick said, looking at Ron.

"I was walking down the hall last week, and I saw Stephen coming out of the file room," Bill said.

"He was in the file room?" Ron asked.

"That's right."

"Where was Connie?" Lydia asked.

"Holding the door open for him. I can't get in the file room because of our internal controls, but Stephen goes in and reviews files."

"Only his own," Nick said quickly.

"How in the hell do you know that?" Bill said. "How can you be so definite? Connie's up at the entrance servicing employees, since they're not allowed in, while he's in the back, looking at whatever he fuckin' feels like. Then he walks out with his briefcase, with who knows what inside."

"He shouldn't be in the file room," Ron said, looking over at Nick.

"Fine. So I'll tell him," Nick hesitated and then continued, glaring at Bill.

"You know, you pick one isolated situation and blow it up."

"This is more than one isolated situation, Nick, and you know it," Bill continued, his eyes fixed on Nick's.

"Who was it that we selected recently as our independent inspector for the Carr and Larson projects?"

Nick rifled back, "John Daletti, one of the most able professionals in Florida."

"Did you know that Stephen and Andrew are friends of Daletti's?"

"How in the hell do you know that?"

"I saw them together outside the West Palm Beach Yacht Club—they looked like pretty good buddies."

"Bullshit!" Nick responded, his face reddening.

"Marie and I were there. We saw them. In fact, we talked to them. They appeared to be pretty chummy."

He probably never even heard of Jason Daletti until Carr or Larson mentioned his name, Bill thought. *And it's his job to make sure the inspectors are independent.*

"So, what are you trying to say, Bill?" Nick asked caustically. "It's now a crime to know someone in the same industry?"

"I'm not saying that, Nick. What I am saying is that the appearance is bad—and maybe there's more to this relationship."

"Fuck you," Nick said coldly.

"So what are your thoughts?" Ron asked, looking over at Casey.

"During our next set of meetings throughout the office, all employees should be reminded that borrowers are only allowed in public areas and in their respective account manager's office. And they really shouldn't leave the reception area without an employee escort."

"That's ridiculous!" Nick said, jerking his head back toward the group.

"Bill's right," Ron interrupted. "I see Stephen and Andrew all over the offices, oftentimes by themselves. That's not good, and I assume part of the blame because I haven't said anything to them.

"On the other hand, there's not much we can do about Jason Daletti at this point. Nick evidently checked him out, and Jason knowing Stephen and Andrew really shouldn't have made a difference in our decision to use him as an inspector—as long as they're not more than acquaintances."

Bill looked at Ron. *He doesn't look like he believes Nick either,* he thought. *Why does he ever believe him?*

"Lydia, who's up?" Ron continued.

"It's Nick's turn."

Nick got up from his chair and closed his eyes. When he reopened them, they appeared to be dancing with excitement.

This guy's unbelievable, Bill thought. *One minute, he's argumentative and short, and the next, he's ready to inform and entertain.*

"I'm very excited about the Alpha Division and some of the inroads we've made in that arena. I would also like any suggestions, as far as new initiatives you think we should explore. Our current efforts are moving along well.

"First of all, our new charter consulting business has been busy, but we are facing some challenges. We have a lot of activity, but because we're dealing with organizations in their embryonic stage, cash remittances have been slow.

"Naturally, Latham Parish is heavily involved with

the legal documentation and the interaction with the regulators.

"The next step, from our standpoint, will be to assist the new companies in selecting their staff, setting up their systems and procedures, and preparing them for their grand opening. We'll need everyone's help at that point."

"Where are these companies located?" Lydia asked.

"We have two here in Palm Beach County that we all know about. Then we have one in South Carolina, two in California, and two in Texas."

"Do we have enough staff for the training and other work?" Lydia continued.

"That's debatable."

"So where are most of these leads coming from?" Bill asked.

Nick looked at Ron and raised his eyebrows. "Latham Parish—it's a great deal for the firm. They pick up new business and charge us for all their expenses—and believe me, they go first class."

"So they go on the road and solicit consulting engagements for us," Bill said.

"That's right," Nick responded halfheartedly, "but there are several problems we have to work out. First of all, Latham Parish gets paid right away, but we don't get compensated until later, after the institution starts to make money. That could be several years."

"Or more," Ron interjected.

"Or more," Nick agreed, nodding his head.

"What about stock options?" Bill asked.

"Granted, in most cases, where we want options in partial payment, we get them. On the other hand, we really don't know if they'll ever have any value.

"Over and above the risk we take on payment, options,

etc., I'm even more concerned about the way we're pushing our staff. Our internal growth is difficult enough to keep up with, but this extra work is really too much for us."

"What about adding more people?" Bill asked.

"Lydia's working with me on that, but we can't hire good people fast enough.

"We really need to slow down Latham Parish-not stop, but certainly slow down."

"Nick Donofrio says we have to slow down. This, I don't believe," Lydia quipped.

"I never thought I'd say it. Not only do they get us too much business, they guarantee the work effort will start immediately. They've given us impossible target dates on several of these engagements, and we just can't do it."

Nick took a deep breath.

"Anyway, as I mentioned, our consulting practice is busy," He said, with a childish look on his face.

Everyone laughed.

"I'll talk to the appropriate people over there," Ron said.

"Thanks," Nick responded.

"Okay, team," Ron said, looking at his watch and down at his agenda. "Lydia's on."

She continued for the remainder of the afternoon, discussing savings programs and personnel policies. The meeting went smoothly, until she started to address training and education.

"Each of our office managers, both savings and lending, will be sent to the Dale Carnegie training program."

"Why?" Nick asked.

Lydia appeared to be caught off guard. "What do you mean why?" She asked, looking at Nick quizzically.

"I think that's a pretty simple question. Why do we plan to send all the office managers to this?...what program?"

"Dale Carnegie," She said, appearing somewhat irritated. "It's an excellent course that teaches a number of things, but basically people and communication skills."

"The lending department will take care of its own people. We know what they need," He said curtly.

"We've got the program in place with the Dale Carnegie franchisee in the area," Ron interrupted. "Bill recommended we use it when he first came on board, and we've found it has worked wonders on several people from the savings offices."

"I don't understand why Lydia and Bill are continually trying to get control of our departments," Nick said, his face becoming taut, while glaring at Bill.

"Everything is bounced off me, and in most cases, you too," Ron said. "If you can give us good reasons why a certain direction we're moving is illogical, that's fine. But don't even bring up the question of turf for turf's sake, Nick. We can't operate that way. This is a team operation."

He stood up and walked over to Nick, who was obviously tense.

"That's the only way it can work. That's what personnel and training departments are for, Nick—for the company.

"It's not logical to have separate support departments for each segment of the business. We've got too much of that as it is."

He continued over to get a cup of coffee, and without turning back toward the group, He said, "Lydia, continue."

She finished her presentation with no additional controversies. By the end of the meeting day, tempers seemed to subside, and the atmosphere was relatively civil.

ॐ

"So how do you think it went?" Lydia asked, as she sat on Bill's office couch.

"Probably better than expected. I mean—it's obvious that Nick's tied into Carr and Larson and probably several other borrowers at some level."

"Do you think Ron feels the same way?" Lydia asked.

"I think so, but he's more indirect with his comments. He told me a few weeks ago that Nick was a 'complicated' personality."

"That's an understatement."

Bill nodded his head. "You know what, Lydia?"

"What?"

"That guy scares me."

༜

The evening was unseasonably pleasant for Washington, D.C. The sky was clear, the temperature was 75 degrees, with very little humidity, and there was a slight breeze.

"Norm, I'd like to introduce you to Ron Jameson and Nick Donofrio from Dawn Savings.

Ron and Nick, Senator Norm Nichols," Ed Marks said.

"I'm very pleased to meet you two gentlemen. Ed has told me a great deal about your company. I'm impressed with what you're doing in the new deregulated environment."

"We appreciate the kind words, Senator," Nick said.

"Without support from people like you, opportunities for companies like ours would be nonexistent," Ron said.

"Well, thank you. And we appreciate you coming all the way to Washington to spend time with us."

"It's our pleasure," Ron answered.

"Ed asked me to bring as many banking committee members as possible. I think we'll have five for the cruise," Senator Nichols said, as he looked up at the boat from the dock.

"It's gorgeous. The *Vagabond*, huh. How big is it?"

"One hundred and twenty feet. I'm not sure of the other dimensions," Ron said, looking around for Stephen or Andrew.

"It has a recreation and dining room, a nice galley, and sleeps six. It's owned by two developers that work with us. They were cruising up the coast anyway, and the timing for this meeting was just perfect.

"They have a great interest in expressing their viewpoints to you and your fellow senators, just as we do."

He hesitated for a few seconds, looking down at the water and then back up at Nichols.

"I have to warn you, Senator, they do have strong opinions."

"One of our most significant responsibilities as members of the Senate is to listen. We're always ready to learn from practitioners."

"I just hope we don't chew your ear off, Norm," Ed Marks added.

"We have a tendency to go on and on when it comes to Dawn Savings and its potential," Nick interjected.

"That's one thing you shouldn't be concerned about. Like I said, we're always accused of Potomac Fever—you know, not really knowing what life outside the Beltway is like. Based upon what I've read and what Ed's told me, I want you to keep doing what you're doing.

"On the other hand, I'm warning you now, not everyone coming tonight feels the way I do."

"That's not a problem," Nick responded intently. "We'd rather meet those who disagree with us. If they're logical people, it won't take long for them to understand our position."

"Well then, tonight we'll all learn firsthand."

"I'm confident of that," Nick responded. "How about a drink and a few snacks before the rest of the guests arrive,"

"I'd love to," the senator replied, as the three men walked to the boat.

"We'll get Stephen and Andrew to give you a complete tour," Nick added.

"Terrific."

"You may be the best thing since bagels and cream cheese, but I constantly receive complaints from my constituents in Palm Beach and Broward counties," Senator Bernstein, an elder statesman from Florida, said to Nick and Ron as the *Vagabond* cruised up the Potomac.

The men were leaning against the guardrail on the main deck, partially mesmerized by the historic river and shoreline.

Nick put his hand on the senator's shoulder. "Are these constituents our customers?"

"Well...a...well, no."

"Do you mind if we ask you who it is that have these complaints, Senator?" Ron questioned.

"No, I don't mind. They came from other banks' and thrifts' executives."

"Our competition," Ron confirmed.

"Yes, I...I guess that's right, your competition."

"Senator, that 'problem' has been with us since we started. We're appreciated by our customers, but not our competition," Nick said.

"That's because you pay higher interest rates than anyone in the area. That's the reason they're upset. You're going to put them and yourselves out of business," Bernstein said, shaking his finger at Nick.

"Is that what they tell you?"

"Why sure. And I see your advertisements in the paper."

"Well, the truth is, Senator, we very seldom, if ever, price our savings programs at the top of the market. We try to stay in the highest rate quartile if we need the money in a specific maturity range, but if you check the paper closely, you'll see that we're not at the top."

"They tell me that when they set their rates where they do, well below you, they can't make a profit—and it's your fault."

"Senator, they don't lose money because of us, they lose it because of themselves," Ron said. "Granted, part of their problem is their portfolio of long-term fixed-rate loans at low average rates.

"I realize they were encouraged by Congress to make those loans in the past, but now you've taken away the protection of a rate ceiling and the differential over the banks on savings rates. That's why they're getting squeezed."

"So why are you different," he asked, scrunching his face.

"Fortunately, we don't have the albatross of the low-yielding, long-term, fixed-rate mortgages around our neck. When we make those types of loans, we sell them in the secondary markets, so we don't retain the risk."

"And that's good?" the Senator asked.

"That's very good," Ron continued. "The mortgages we do keep have adjustable features that rise and fall with rates in general. The interesting glitch, that our competition probably fails to bring to your attention, is that even though the loans they've made for years are killing them, and the government protection they've had in the past is now practically nonexistent, their modus operandi hasn't changed. They're still making and holding their loans in inventory, instead of selling, to reduce their risk."

Berstein looked surprised. "Why would they do that?"

Nick raised his arms and eyebrows and said, "We have no idea."

"I guess they fully expect the American people to bail them out of any future problems they may have," Ron interjected.

"We don't. They're squeezed, and can't pay a reasonable rate to your constituents. But most of our customers are retirees, and they come to us for reasons over and above our rates."

"Such as?"

"We cater to their every banking need," Nick answered.

"We treat them like gold," Ron added.

"You know, Senator, we can go on and on about Dawn, but talk is cheap. The best way for you to understand our company is to see our people, and your constituents, in action. When's the next time you'll be coming to Florida?"

"Over the holiday recess in a few weeks."

"Would you spend a half day with us?"

"We know you'll be impressed," Nick added.

"Sure, why not."

"I'll have my secretary work out a day and time with your office," Ron said.

"I'm looking forward to the firsthand education. As I said, all I've heard are rumors up until now, and they haven't been good."

"I wouldn't guess they would be," Ron said, smiling. "But we'll tell you exactly how we do things and why."

"Terrific," the Senator said.

"Would you excuse me for a few minutes, gentlemen? I told Stephen that I'd catch up with him about now."

"Sure," Bernstein said. "Nick can tell me a little more about your operation. Kind of a preview before my visit."

"My pleasure," Nick said.

Ron went below two steps to the walnut-trimmed recreation room and saw Stephen snacking off one of the beautifully decorated party trays.

Stephen looked up. "So you said something earlier about trying to cover Washington from several different angles. What else are you doing?"

"Bill Casey spent part of last week with the regulators trying to convince them to give us the benefit of the doubt."

"On what?"

"On everything."

"So how did he do?"

"Well, it's really hard to say. He used to work for the agency, and they seem to have respect for him. Only time will tell."

Ron dipped a large piece of shrimp in the cocktail sauce, and took a bite. "This is good," He said.

"So what do you think about today so far, Stephen?" Ron asked, as he looked through the portholes at the slow changing shoreline and then back up at the groups conversing on deck.

"I think it was a great idea," Stephen said. "Of course," he continued, nudging Ron's arm, "since it was mine, how could it be anything else?"

"No question about it," Ron said, grinning. "It was just the entrée we needed—Ed's connection and your yacht... what a combination. And with five of them and five of us, no one feels overpowered.

"We have to convince the distinguished senators that eliminating tax breaks for the real estate industry could be a disaster for the economy."

"That's an understatement," Stephen said, intently. "Just discussions about these possible tax law changes on Capitol Hill are killing our syndication sales."

"That's what I understand.

"Listen, I don't know if Nick's talked to you yet, but we'll be more than happy to assist your financial and marketing people in looking at alternatives to syndication sales. We're in this together, and if you don't sell, it hurts both our organizations."

"No, he hasn't offered us assistance, but we'd appreciate some help, thanks."

Stephen's head turned as he glanced back and up at the main deck.

"Did you meet Senator Canton from Texas?" He asked.

"Not yet."

"Great guy. Andrew has him cornered out there. I told him earlier that Dawn was already in Texas, and that Andrew and I will be joining you there soon. He loves real estate developers and oil people. Come on—I'll introduce you," Stephen said, putting his arm around Ron and ushering him up to meet the Senator.

Chapter 9

Jake Fleshman laid in a lounge chair at the edge of his pool. The sun was hot, but there was a slight breeze.

"Hey, Jake," Larry Fleshman called as he opened the gate and walked across the pool deck. He was wearing long surfing style trunks, togs, sunglasses and a California tan. With no response, he tapped his older brother's sunglasses.

"Time for work, oh man among men."

Jake stirred, stretched his body, slowly sat up, and looked at his brother.

"You can be a real pain in the ass."

"I know I can, but that's what makes me special. Special enough to be your sibling."

Larry sat down on a chair next to the chaise. He stretched his legs and leaned his head on a built-in cushion on the back of the chair, closing his eyes.

"So, to what do I owe this visit on a Sunday afternoon?"

Larry opened his eyes and looked toward his brother.

"Well, as you know, Larry Fleshman never sleeps. He's constantly looking for new opportunities to make the family some money."

"Terrific. What's the opportunity?"

Larry sat up with renewed energy.

"Do you remember the realtor from Florida I talked to you about last year?"

"Slightly."

"I met him in a bar on Singer Island. Anyway, I told him what we do and gave him my card."

"This is all very interesting, but as you noticed, I was extremely busy when you dropped in. If you don't mind, I'm going get back to an important part of my Sunday afternoon," Jake said, as he rolled over, turning away from Larry.

Without hesitation, Larry got up out of his chair, grabbed the edge of the chaise with both hands, and threw his brother and the lounge chair into the pool.

Immediately, Larry jumped in the water and grabbed his brother's shoulders as he came to the surface.

"Are you listening to me, man?" He said, raising his voice and looking at his brother with a devilish smile.

"I am now," Jake answered, wiping the water out of eyes.

Jake's wife, Nadia, walked out of the house to the edge of the pool.

"I don't believe you two—you're like kids," She said, her hands on her hips.

Larry thought for a few seconds, grinning. "You married into a strange family, Nadia."

"I guess so. Can I trust you two out here alone, or will the neighbors end up calling the police for disturbing the peace?"

Larry took a deep breath. "I'll try to control myself," He said as she walked back into the house.

"So, let's get back to this important business," Jake said, curtly, leaning against the side of the pool.

"What about this realtor?"

"He called me."

"That's terrific; and what did he say?"

"Well, there's a company that's traded over-the-counter, Dawn Savings and Loan, that he thinks we should keep our eye on."

"We've never done a financial institution before."

"That's the first time I've ever heard you say that. We've never done this," He said, raising his eyebrows.

"Do you think that maybe you're getting a little too old for this business?" Larry continued, twisting his head to the side, grinning.

"Fine," Jake responded, waving his arms. "Why should we keep an eye on this company?"

"He said they're making some questionable loans. Basically land acquisition, development, and construction types—they're referred to as ADCs. Dawn has been making these loans to less than top-shelf borrowers. They put very little, if any, money in the deal. The theory is that they add their expertise and supervision—they call it 'sweat equity'—and that the lender supplies the cash."

"And?" Jake asked, appearing disinterested.

"And," Larry responded with great emphasis, "I think the risk is substantial!" he continued, raising his voice.

"Now, Dawn gets something called 'additional consideration' or 'equity kickers', besides its rate and fees—they call it merchant banking—but I question whether that outweighs the negatives."

"Define those terms for me, Larry." Jake's interest appeared piqued.

"They both mean the same thing. The lending institution shares in the profits with the developer, so, I guess that's why Dawn feels it's worth the risk. But you know what the real estate market is like—it's crazy."

Jake nodded. "So that's why you're hot on this situation."

"That alone would make me want to sell this company's stock short, but there's a second issue that's really frosting on the cake. The relationship really sounds like a joint venture, like a partnership."

"Now you're really starting to bore me, brother."

Larry moved to the corner of the pool at the shallow end. He sat on the steps and leaned back, closing his eyes and stretching his arms along the edges.

Jake looked at his brother and shook his head. "I hate when you think you've got something hot."

"Well, first of all," He said, leaning forward and opening his eyes. "I don't think I've got something hot—I know. As I mentioned, these are not top-shelf borrowers."

"I heard that the first time."

"These ADC loans comprise over 60 percent of Dawn's portfolio. And even though these things sound like partnerships, or joint ventures, they're all recorded as loans."

Jake moved forward from the pool's edge, toward his brother.

"I may be thick, but I still don't understand the significance."

"Well, from an accounting standpoint, it's a gray area that's starting to get closer to black. The method for recording that type of transaction is under a lot of scrutiny by the various accounting authorities, especially the Financial Accounting Standards Board.

"Right now, the rules allow some of the fees to be recognized, along with income from the interest reserves they set up as part of the loan. When 60 percent of your assets are these types of loans, that's a lot of fees and interest."

"So what's the alternative the Standards Board is looking at?" Jake asked.

"They'd consider it a joint venture, which really means that income could only be recognized after the sale of the property takes place."

"The difference in income, now versus later in the case of Dawn, would have to be substantial," Jake added.

Larry put his hand on his brother's shoulder. "You're smarter than you look.

"But the real beauty of this situation is that it's a triple whammy. Their borrowers are not the best, they have a tremendous number of dollars out there in these transactions, and the authorities could pull the rug out from under their accounting treatment, resulting in a major income adjustment."

"Would they make this adjustment retroactive?" Jake asked, slowly smiling.

"I don't know, but can you imagine the hit they'd take in the market even if only their future transactions were recorded in the more conservative fashion...with as much volume as they've got? Unbelievable!"

"When are you going to Florida?"

"Tomorrow morning. I set up a meeting with their chief financial officer—a guy named Bill Casey. I told him I was a potential investor. I'm supposed to meet several of the senior officers and look at some of their projects. I mean," Larry hesitated, "this situation looks almost perfect, but I want to make sure."

"This does sound like one of our deals, Larry."

"Jake...I can taste it."

"May I help you please?"

"Yes. I'm here to see Bill Casey. My name is Larry Fleshman."

"Did you have an appointment, Mr. Fleshman?"

"Yes, ma'am."

"Please have a seat, and I'll let Mr. Casey know you're here."

Larry looked around the reception area—prints depicting Florida; frames, a chair and couch trimmed in dark wood, with upholstery in dark blue with a light blue shell pattern. Banking conservative, but definitely Florida. Nothing ostentatious.

A young lady with blonde hair and a bright smile bounced down the hall toward him. She held out her hand.

"Mr. Fleshman, I'm Cathy Demming, Mr. Casey's secretary. If you follow me, I'll take you back to his office."

"Thank you, Ms. Demming."

They walked through the two-story building, down a long hallway. They exchanged pleasantries about his trip and Florida before she stopped and opened a set of doors that appeared to be the executive area.

There were approximately ten to twelve people deeply involved in their work—some at their word processors, some moving between four offices, and others on the telephone.

She walked to the office at the far end of the section and knocked lightly on the partially closed door.

"Bill, I have Mr. Fleshman with me."

"Come on in."

Larry followed Cathy into the office, and Bill Casey extended his hand, walking out from behind his desk.

"I hope you had a nice trip, Larry."

"I did, Bill," Larry said, following the lead, and introducing himself informally. "Thank you."

"Can we get you a cup of coffee? Or better yet, some orange juice? You know you're in Florida."

"I'd love some juice."

"Bill, I'll get it."

"Thanks, Cathy," He said, as she left the office.

"She seems nice, Bill," Larry said.

"Oh, she's really an asset to this company," He said, looking over at Larry. "She works hard; she's bright and also very personable."

Larry was nodding his head in agreement. "You don't find that combination too often."

"You know," Bill paused for a second, "in the past, I would have agreed with you, but not here. We're very fortunate."

"Well, if Cathy's any indication of the type of people you have here, I agree with you wholeheartedly."

"Did I hear my name in vain?" Cathy asked, as she entered the room with a glass of juice.

"Larry was just telling me what a fantastic impression you made on him, as a first-time visitor to Dawn."

"I get that from my boss," Cathy said, smiling as she turned and left, pulling the door shut.

"I've got you scheduled for a pretty full day," Bill said, looking down at a list. "We'll spend some time together," he continued, "and then I'll have you talk to Lydia Lewis, our senior officer in charge of Savings Operations, Personnel, and Advertising—she's excellent. If our employees get their lead for a positive attitude and a caring work ethic from anyone, it's from Lydia.

"After that, you'll have lunch with Ron Jameson. Then, Nick Donofrio, our top lending guy, will take you for an hour or so helicopter trip, so you can observe some of our borrowers' projects firsthand. You'll see more in an hour than if you drove around for a day."

"That sounds great."

"First for an overview of the organization," Bill began.

Ron and Larry ordered and had just finished discussing the benefits of Florida and California living when their food arrived.

"Based upon what I've seen, Lydia and Bill are certainly two of Dawn's most significant assets," Larry said, above the noise of the restaurant.

"I agree. People make it happen in the service industries, and since I hired them both, I'm very pleased.

"And the nice thing about good leaders is that they attract other good people. I can't tell you the number of individuals that have joined Dawn because they worked with or knew one of those two before."

"They speak highly of you."

"I would hope so," Ron responded with a smile.

"So what are your plans as far as the business? Where do you plan to go?"

"Well, as you undoubtedly know, outside the state of Florida, we have loan origination offices in Texas and Arizona. Those three states are really all we need for the immediate future, as far as our lending operation.

"Up until six months ago, we only had savings offices on the east coast of this state. At that point, we purchased Thomas Jefferson Savings, a small state-chartered institution headquartered in Tallahassee with four offices. We really weren't interested in Tallahassee, so we merged the two offices we wanted into our organization and put the remaining corporate structure with two offices up for sale. The closing took place recently."

"So, financially, how did the deal turn out?"

Slowly, a smile came to Ron's face.

"We bought the franchise with the branch offices for three million, stripped out the two we wanted, and sold the franchise and Tallahassee offices for five million."

"Not a bad deal, not a bad deal at all."

"We'd like to do a couple of those every year."

"I bet you would," Larry said. "What else is on the agenda for Dawn?"

"We have another purchase in St. Augustine—Desoto Savings. It'll be a straight acquisition and merger."

"How big is it?"

"Three hundred fifty million and six offices—perfect for us."

"Anything else?"

"Well, generally, the Alpha Division."

"The Alpha Division?" Larry questioned, shaking his head.

"That's right. It's our research and development group that tries to continually keep us moving forward for everyone's benefit: the stockholders, the customers, the employees—Dawn, in total."

"That's kind of unusual in this business, isn't it?"

"It is, but then Dawn isn't the traditional, stodgy, run-of-the-mill financial institution either."

"From what I've seen, I couldn't agree with you more."

"From a more practical standpoint, we sold Thomas Jefferson for several reasons.

"Our counsel tells us that legally, in order to accomplish some of our long-term goals, our best operating structure is a unitary holding company. Evidently, the interpretation allows Dawn to be the holding company, with one thrift or banking subsidiary, but not both.

"As we mentioned in our last 10Q, we have an offer outstanding to buy a very small bank just outside Tucson, so we really had to sell Thomas Jefferson. Other than Florida, there's no better savings state than Arizona."

"I did read about Arizona, although I understand there

are some pretty healthy roadblocks to completing that acquisition."

"Sure there are, but that's exactly the challenge we need to keep our juices flowing. We work with obstacles every day. Maybe it's not possible in our current regulatory environment, but if anyone can do it, we will."

Ron looked at his watch. "I can't believe we've talked for almost two hours."

"The time flew—you've been very interesting."

"Well, your whirlwind tour with Nick should be even more so. Let's go."

They drove back to the office, and Ron pointed out some of the nearby shopping center projects Dawn had financed. The centers were all busy and appeared to be fully occupied.

They walked into Ron's office.

"Let me go round up Nick, and I'll be back in a few minutes. If you need anything, ask Sylvia."

"Terrific," Larry responded, forcing a smile. *This trip may have been a mistake*, he thought.

Bill looked up from his desk as Ron hurried into his office.

"How was lunch?"

"Great. I have Larry in reception. Did you brief Nick as far as his tour with Larry?"

"Sure, but I really can't be sure how much good it did, coming from me. You'd better give him some guidance."

"I understand."

Ron walked through the executive wing and stepped into Nick's office.

"Are you all set for Larry Fleshman's tour?"

"No sweat," Nick answered quickly. "By the time we come back, he'll be ready to buy a ton of our stock. I'll razzle-dazzle the man."

"Don't go overboard. He's no hayseed. On the contrary, he seems very perceptive. He knows more about our business than you'd think."

"Did Bill suggest you come see me?"

"Sure," Ron answered, with no hesitancy. "Bill's concerned about Larry's overall feeling about us. He's the CFO, and market perception is one of his responsibilities. I feel exactly the same way."

Shaking his head and wincing slightly, Nick said, "Please tell Bill that before he came here, market perception was my responsibility, and I think I know what to do and what not to do."

"I said that perception is part of his job, and he's right in being concerned. He works with the market every day, and he usually knows what makes it feel good and what sets it off—even the most innocent actions."

"Fine," Nick responded curtly. "I won't embarrass the company."

"Thank you," Ron said, turning on his heels and walking back to his office.

"He's ready," Ron said to Larry, as he walked into the reception area.

"It looks like the helicopter's out in the yard."

Larry walked over to the window.

"Yeah, I watched it land. Do you own the helicopter, or do you rent it whenever it's necessary?"

Ron joined him at the window.

"Actually, we own it. It's part of our inventory. We have an aircraft brokerage and sales subsidiary."

"I know you didn't mention anything about that sub in your last 10K or annual report."

"You're right," Ron said, nodding his head. "The company's new. We started less than two months ago."

"Airplane brokerage and sales is kind of unusual for a financial institution. Did this originate from your Alpha Division?"

"No, not exactly. Even though it's a relatively new company, the concept evolved some time ago. But the process that gave birth to the aircraft subsidiary was really the impetus for the research and development effort that went into what we now call Alpha."

"So how productive has your think tank been?"

"We've reviewed hundreds of situations thus far. As long as we don't violate the regulations and there's some potential, we'll try it. Our approach to that environment is basically one of omission."

"Omission? I don't understand," Larry said, raising his eyebrows.

"I guess I should clarify. We don't wait for the regulators to say we can do something before we do it. If there's a void, we can fill it at a profit, and the regs don't say we can't, we may give it a shot. In this case, we started when we picked up a twin prop as additional consideration on a loan we made last year."

"I did read about the additional consideration. If I understand it correctly, it's extra compensation you get for making the loan, over and above the interest and fees."

"That's exactly right—why don't we sit down," Ron said as he headed for the couch back in his office. "I thought Nick would be here by now." He looked at Larry and smiled. "Some of our customers call it our 'vigorish.'"

"Vigorish?"

"That's correct," Ron said, as they sat. "It's a Yiddish word that means, 'a little extra,'" He said, rubbing his forefinger and thumb together.

"Usually it comes to us in the form of cash, but often we receive it in some other medium—for instance, the twin-engine airplane I mentioned. We made a loan on a fly-in, fly-out residential development for people who own or lease aircraft and want to be nearby for transportation purposes, or because flying is a significant pastime activity."

"So there's actually a landing strip in the development?"

"Exactly. In that type of development, the strip is typically only grass, but that's really all you need for a small plane. Anyway, the borrower is a developer and an aircraft salesman. It was less expensive for him to give us the additional consideration in a plane at the wholesale value than if he paid us in cash. We gave him credit at retail."

"Very interesting. I have a few more questions about the concept, but you were telling me about how you got into the aircraft sales business."

"Right. After we acquired the plane, we needed a pilot. I heard about a young guy who had flown jet aircraft in Saudi Arabia for a shake.

"He came back to this country, got his broker's and contractor's licenses and built and sold a few houses.

"Anyway, I called him, we got along well, and I hired him. He was a junior loan officer and flew when we needed him to get us somewhere quickly.

"A few months ago, he suggested we get into the aircraft brokerage business. He actually put together a relatively sophisticated proposal. Since it was only brokerage, there was minimal initial investment."

"How have you done?" Larry asked.

"We did quite well over the initial sixty to ninety days—sold several aircraft. He suggested we could do even better if we had a few used units in inventory. So now we own two jet aircraft, a Lear and a Hawker. We also have the helicopter out in the yard. They're all for sale, but if necessary, we use them."

"What about that initial twin?"

Ron smiled. "We sold it—at a profit. I love when things come together."

They both laughed.

Larry sat up in his chair. "What else have you accepted as this additional consideration besides cash and an airplane? Give me another example."

I feel like a wet dishrag, Ron thought. *This guy's wearing me out. Where in the hell is Nick?*

"Most anything. For instance, we deal with a borrower, who has several businesses, one of those being selling and leasing cars. Besides our interest and fees, we received two of our company cars, a Jaguar and a Mercedes, as part of the cost of the loan."

"I guess the concern I had when I read about this," Larry said, hesitating, "is why would a borrower be willing to give you these extra monies, in whatever form, over and above your interest and fees?"

"That's a good question," Ron said.

"Most developers typically aren't flush with cash, but they do have inventory of some type. Their monies come in when they sell a unit, lot, etc.

"We recognize that cash flow problem, and allow them to build interest and fees into the loan, if the appraisal warrants it.

"And, in addition, the interest we charge is lower than it should be, considering the risk factor, so the additional consideration makes up the difference for both."

"The average interest rate on your portfolio appears relatively high even without that added differential."

Ron smiled, weakly. "You're right, Larry. It's a healthy average, but it should be higher. The development business is risky, but it's also been around forever."

Larry moved forward in his seat. "But you've also mentioned that most of your borrowers are of the class B and C variety. That's certainly another reason for the high rates. They probably can't get loans anywhere else."

Ron stood up, took a deep breath, looked down the empty hallway and then focused back on Larry.

"Their options are more limited than an A borrower, I'd agree, but they certainly have other alternatives."

Larry leaned back. "Your percentage of admittedly 'risky' ADC loans concerns me, Ron. It looks like you've got all your eggs in one basket."

"Our ADC loans make up more of our portfolio than we would like, but we're in the process of reducing that percentage.

"Currently, I have no great concern. Our underwriting, compliance, and project monitoring are second to none, and our people responsible for that area are the reason I feel as comfortable as I do."

The door to Ron's office was open, and Nick walked in.

"Sylvia said you were waiting for me, so I didn't bother to knock."

"No problem—I thought you were lost."

"I picked up a telephone call I shouldn't have," Nick said.

"That's fine. Happens to the best of us," Ron responded, smiling.

"Larry Fleshman, this is Nick Donofrio, chief lending officer.

"Nick, this is Larry Fleshman, hopefully a future investor in our stock."

Larry stood and shook hands with Nick.

"My pleasure," Nick said. "Well, the chopper's ready. I'll show you some of our borrowers' projects and answer any questions you have about our lending policies and procedures," he continued, leading the way.

"Ron, I'll see you later," Larry said on his way out the door with Nick.

"I'll be here," Ron responded. He smiled and waved. As soon as they were out of his office, he fell back into his chair, closing his eyes.

The helicopter landed back at Dawn's headquarters. Larry and Nick stepped down from the cab and started to walk across the grass field toward the building. Larry turned as soon as the noise from the rotating blades was no longer overwhelming.

"I really appreciate the time you spent with me, Nick."

"Any time. I hope I was able to answer all your questions and help you arrive at a conclusion."

"This morning, I was unclear as far as my direction, but now there's no question. I believe my family and I will do extremely well with your stock."

"That's great! If you need any more information about our borrowers or their projects, let us know."

"Bill," Larry called, as he knocked on Casey's door.

"Come on in."

"Interesting tour," Larry said, as he walked into the room quickly.

"I tried to thank Ron, but he was tied up with an appointment, and I really would like to get to the airport soon to catch the next plane back home. You don't mind do you?"

"Certainly not," Bill responded, getting up.

"But I'd also like to use a telephone for a few minutes."

"No problem. I'll go back and get one of our guys to take you. Sit down and use my phone," Bill said, as he walked out the door.

"Hello."

"Jake."

"Larry."

"I think I hit the jackpot."

"Tell me more," Jake begged.

"This morning I thought that my realtor friend made a shallow assessment of Dawn. If anything my inclination would have been to take a long position."

"But you changed your mind."

"You betcha, big brother. What a change an afternoon can make."

"What should we do?"

Larry hesitated. "We'll talk tomorrow. I'm going to make a few calls at the airport."

"Sounds like it's been a thought-provoking trip."

"Life is beautiful. Stop by tomorrow morning, and I'll tell you about it.

Ciao."

Chapter 10

Bill and Ron were reviewing the most recent annual report in the boardroom. The door was partially open and Nick lightly knocked and proceeded in. His smile was broad.

"What's with you?" Ron asked. "All our delinquent loan customers pay off?"

"No. I just think it's funny that all of you couldn't impress Larry Fleshman yesterday," Nick said, smirking. "It took our lending practices to turn his head."

"Why, what did he say?" Ron asked.

"He said that he wasn't sure what direction to take until he talked to me."

"Well, I hope he decides to buy soon. Our stock went down this morning," Ron said.

"Did you follow it up with anyone?" Bill asked.

"Merrill," Ron said. "Evidently there were quite a few shares sold. Why don't you check with our other market makers and see if you can find out anything?"

"Sure."

Jake walked onto Larry's patio, a combination picnic area, swimming pool deck and portable office. He was already on the speakerphone, squinting at the computer screen that was only partially shaded by a large table umbrella.

"That's what I said, Al. I don't believe the regulators let them get away with that kind of superficial underwriting. They don't know what the word means, for God's sake.

I was just calling you because you had mentioned that you had a small investment in Dawn, and..." Larry listened for a minute or two.

"Oh, it's not that small," Larry added sympathetically. "Well, maybe I'm wrong. I was only there a day. Ask around. Sure. Good. I'll talk to you soon. Good luck."

Larry flicked off the speakerphone and looked at his brother, smiling.

Jake sat down on one of the porch chairs. "So how's Al?"

Larry's eyes glistened, but He said matter-of-factly, "He was fine until a few minutes ago. Now he's shitting in his pants."

"So how do you know their underwriting is superficial? Educated guess?"

"You got it." Larry said, getting out of his chair and walking toward his brother. "I mean, I really don't know anything about their underwriting, but they're so caught up in what they're doing, they aren't even rational. Their biggest mistake is expecting that inflationary increases in real estate values will bail them out of questionable lending.

"I couldn't believe some of the chief lending officer's comments, or his ego." He shook his head.

"Did you call all of Al's friends yet?"

"You know I did, big brother," Larry said.

He lightly slapped Jake on the top of his head and started bouncing around with his fists up like a boxer.

"And, it's just the beginning."

"Ron, do you have a few minutes?" Bill asked, walking into his office.

"Sure. What's going on?"

"Well, I checked with our market makers. There was quite a bit of selling yesterday, and it's continuing today. So I did a little research." Bill hesitated.

"And?"

"And, Larry Fleshman and his brother Jake are evidently small, but well respected short-sellers."

Ron sat up in his chair, straightening the papers on his desk. His face started to turn crimson.

"Damn," he yelled, slamming his fist on the desk. "We should have checked them out."

"I know. I take the responsibility for that," Bill said.

"We've got enough problems from our borrowers.

"Now the short-sellers are going to be all over our asses."

He got up from his chair and walked toward the window, with his hands clasped behind his back, looking at the helicopter pick-up area.

"Evidently, Nick really impressed Fleshman, huh? Asshole. I can just imagine what he told him.

"Listen," he turned around and looked at Bill, "from now on, no one gets in here to talk to our people until you thoroughly investigate who they are."

Bill was looking at the floor, visibly embarrassed.

"You know," He said, "the stock was moving so well, I guess I got careless. I should have checked him out when he asked to visit, but I didn't even think..." Bill hesitated.

"I've already sent out a memo explaining that all requests for future visits by any current or perspective shareholders or anyone else we're not familiar with be directed to our financial public relations firm for screening."

He hesitated momentarily.

"We've been impressing people until now."

"We've been—you and I, but we haven't really exposed anyone else to the marketplace, until now, and it was probably a mistake on my part."

"No—it was my mistake. A short-seller never should have gotten in here. I didn't do my homework."

"Listen, Bill, if it wasn't these Fleshman brothers, it would be somebody else. I mean, anyone can sell a stock short, even people that are traditionally long.

"If they don't like what someone here said, or if the industry is in the tank, even one of our so-called friends could take a negative position. Unfortunately, that's part of being a public company."

Bill looked up at Ron and managed a weak smile.

"Thanks for the compassion, but that's not all the bad news."

Ron sat back in his chair. "What?"

"The Fleshman brothers have been known to get on a stock and jump hard. I mean, they'll do whatever's necessary to depress it."

"Like what?"

"Well, evidently they pass a lot of rumors around, many of which start with them. Naturally, they're untrue or exaggerated."

"What the hell does NASDAQ do about that kind of activity? There must be some type of policing that goes on."

"I'm not sure what they do, but I'll find out. I may be going overboard on this—we still don't know how serious they are."

"It doesn't matter. Like I said, if it's not them, it would be someone else. Let's learn all we can about NASDAQ short-seller rules, regulations, policy, etc.

"We're going to have to generate even more enthusiasm in our stock to overcome potential negative rumors."

Ron hesitated for a few seconds. "Any money in the profit-sharing plan that we're authorized to use for stock purchases?"

"Some."

"Good, let's do it. And we may have to go to the board and other senior officers and ask them to buy more. We'll offer them lines of credit if they need the cash."

"There are a few things they can do over and above buying more that won't necessitate any additional cash or borrowings on their part," Bill said.

"Like?"

"I know some of the guys have purchased stock on margin in the aftermarket, and may have it registered in 'street name.'"

"In the name of the broker-dealer they do business with?"

"Right. Unfortunately, if that's the case, the broker-dealer can lend the stock without the owner's permission to someone like the Fleshmans."

"And then they short it," Ron answered, staring at the ceiling. "So our board, or for that matter any of our shareholders that have margined stock in their broker-dealers' name, may be working against themselves."

"That's right. And naturally, the broker-dealer gets compensation in some fashion for lending the stock—the owner gets nothing."

"So let's get that word out to the directors and employees. We'll also try to encourage them to talk to their friends."

"I'll get right on it," Bill said.

"And see if you can come up with any other ideas. Call some of your contacts from other public companies and ask them what they've done, as far as defensive measures."

"Maybe we'll get the Fleshman's in a little short squeeze," Bill said, turning to leave.

"We can certainly try."

The telephone in Nick's office rang.

"Nick Donofrio."

"Nick, this is Ron. I'm over in Sarasota, but I wanted to call and talk for a few minutes."

"What's up?"

"The Fleshmans are up."

Nick stretched back in his chair and smiled broadly.

"So they're buying like crazy, huh. I could have told you that. Larry must have really been impressed with the helicopter tour and our conversation. Do you know how many shares they've bought?"

"The important and incorrect word here is bought, Nick. They didn't buy, they sold."

Nick sat up erect in his chair.

"What do you mean, sold? Did they own shares before Larry's visit?"

"No. They're short sellers."

"Damn. Why didn't Bill know about this?"

"He probably should have. He pointed that out to me yesterday. On the other hand, an investor on one day could be a short seller the next, depending how he or she feels about a company's prospects."

Nick hesitated, "I didn't say anything different to Larry than I say to anyone that asks about our company."

There was no response.

"Did you hear what I said? I didn't..."

"I heard what you said," Ron interrupted. "I've got to catch a plane. Let's talk a little more when I get back."

There was a knock, and the conference room door immediately opened. Nick moved into the room quickly and closed the door behind him—all in one fluid movement.

Bill noticed that he was disheveled, as always, but he also appeared uneasy, and he was carrying what appeared to be a small gift bag. Ron glanced up, but only for a split second, and then continued to review his work.

"So how'd the meeting go with the good Doctor Oro?"

"Well," Nick said hesitantly, "good and not so good."

Ron looked up curiously. "What does that mean?"

Nick appeared nervous and he was sweating profusely. With the door closed, the smell was obnoxious.

"We had a nice time on his yacht. We talked about the relationship."

"That sounds positive," said Ron, as he played with his pencil.

Nick was toying with the bag.

"So, where'd you get that?" Ron asked.

"From Oro."

"What's in it?"

"I don't know—I haven't looked yet," Nick said, sheepishly.

"You drove all the way from Miami and you haven't looked yet? Why?"

"I'm a little concerned at what I'll find. Dr. Oro handed this to me just before I left and said that it was a small token of his appreciation.

"When I tried to give the bag back to him, He said that he wanted me to have it, and that if I didn't take the gift, he would be embarrassed and hurt. He said he wasn't giving me this for business purposes, but rather for friendship."

"Open it," Ron said, tersely.

Nick pulled a felt box from the bag and a gold Presidential

Rolex watch out of the box. After he saw what it was, he appeared almost relieved.

"You've got to return it," Bill said.

Nick jerked his head toward Bill. "Didn't you hear what I said? Dr. Oro would be humiliated if I returned the watch. This is the way Latins operate."

"Nick," Bill responded. "That may be the way Oro operates, but it's wrong and short-sighted for you to accept the gift. You have to give it back—for your own protection."

"Nick, he's right."

"I can't discuss this anymore today," Nick responded. "Neither of you are listening to what I'm saying." He walked out of the office, leaving the watch on the table.

જી

"A gold Rolex watch—you're not serious?" Marie said.

"Honey, this guy's a loose cannon," Bill responded, pacing to one end of the living room and then the other. "And that's only the tip of the iceberg. He's rationalized his actions. He doesn't think he's doing anything wrong. Nick makes me nervous."

"What does Ron say?" She asked, leaning forward on the couch, her hands folded.

"Nothing—at least not to me. I think he's trying to keep peace. All I get are comments about Nick being a complicated personality, whatever that means."

"I had a feeling something like this was going to happen. You should have stayed with Palm."

Bill stopped pacing and he looked down at Marie. "I knew you'd say, 'I told you so.'"

Marie stood up, fixing her eyes on his. "I told you this move was too risky. Now your career—and our family's future—are in jeopardy," She said, walking out of the room.

I set myself up for that, he thought, shaking his head, *but she's right.*

"I can't believe it! Dawn is picking up. How in the hell could there be buying?" Larry groused.

"They probably know that we're selling by now, and Casey figured out who we are. Maybe they're trying to squeeze us a little," Jake responded.

"Time to make a few more calls."

"So what's the story this time?"

"Jameson's father-in-law is involved in drugs in Columbia," Larry said, matter-of-factly.

Jake swung around in his chair, and looked at his brother. "I know you're not serious."

Without hesitation, Larry responded, "I've never been more serious in my life."

His expression was somber, but there was a hint of a smile escaping.

"When I was in Florida, Ron told me that his wife's father was going to visit Columbia over the next several months on one of those exchange programs for businessmen. And he's a pharmacist."

Jake shook his head. "You fox, you. I'm always amazed at your creativity."

"Thank you. Thank you. Thank you," he repeated, as he picked up the phone.

"Damn it!" Larry Fleshman yelled, slamming the table with his fist. "Look at that, Jake."

Jake looked at the screen. "Dawn seems to be holding its' own."

"After I started that rumor about Jameson's father-in-law, it lost a few bucks, but they must be buying."

"So we're either going to take a big loss, or we don't deliver."

"We don't deliver," Larry said with no hesitation, still staring at the screen. "Norton-Steele will cover for us. They don't want to lose our business, no matter what the rules are."

"What about NASDAQ?" Jake said.

"Fuck NASDAQ," Larry responded, looking up at his brother. "What have they done in other situations when we couldn't buy and cover? Nothing."

"We've been lucky."

"I don't think so. They can't follow our transactions through the clearinghouse. Their system's not as sophisticated as they think it is."

"How much time do you think we can get from Norton-Steele?" Jake asked.

"Thirty to sixty days, maybe more."

"Is that enough?"

"I don't know. I'll start more rumors, but what we really need is some negative news from them."

Larry stopped pacing and looked at his brother. "I'm telling you, their lending operation is a disaster waiting to happen."

He started to leave and turned. "I'm going to talk to my guy in Florida—he's had enough time to get us what we need."

"Well, I hope this disaster—whatever it is—happens sooner rather than later."

Larry turned, pointing at Jake. "If it's not in the cards

internally at Dawn, we'll make it happen. It'll be a self-fulfilling prophecy, and we'll look like soothsayers."

Ron walked through the doorway to his office suite. Sylvia handed him his telephone messages and followed him with coffee and juice, setting them down on his desk and politely leaving. The rest of his senior management team was waiting.

Without hesitating, Ron began, "Lydia, you're up first today. How are we doing?"

"Terrific. The Delray and Sun City offices will be open in the next couple of months. Since we're using the same prototype we've used on all our freestanding offices, we've created a big recognition factor with our customers, and we're saving a ton of money on architectural fees."

"Great. Anything else?"

"If there are no objections, in a few weeks, I'd like to make a presentation to the group on a new sales incentive program for our employees."

"Let's do it," Ron said. "Nick, why don't you update us on the exam?"

"Well," Nick answered, "the examiners aren't very happy with our ADC portfolio. They don't understand our lending philosophy, and since we still had some interest reserves built into the loans as of the exam date, we weren't technically delinquent on most of our portfolio.

"Now, they're in a quandary. All they can do at this point is write us up on our documentation and procedures."

"Nick," Ron said, squinting, "we need to spend some time on the credits that are running out of interest reserve and why, but first let's discuss the documentation problem.

"You and I talked about getting all that together, along

with appropriate procedures, before we actually started generating significant ADC loans. If we had done that, we'd be clean at this point."

"I know. I've just been real busy putting deals together."

"There's no excuse. I realize how important generating income is, but you're putting the cart before the horse. Get the documentation and procedures done...and make sure we use them. I'll call Senator Nichols and his friends to help us keep the regulators at bay as long as possible."

"Fine."

"Anything else?" Ron asked.

"Yeah, a couple of things, good and not so good. First, I'm glad that we did very little business with Dr. Oro," He said, looking down and appearing embarrassed.

"Why?"

"He was indicted this morning for mail fraud, racketeering, money laundering, and bank fraud, among other things.

"As we discussed, I knew the Justice Department was conducting an investigation, but I guess this crystallizes his participation in illegal activities."

"So how much business did we do with him?" Bill asked.

"A few miscellaneous deals, but nothing of any significance. Mostly end loans for some of his customers. Anyway, they were underwritten well. I checked just before the meeting. They're still current."

Nick took a deep breath and wiped perspiration off his forehead.

"I'm still working on our Arizona bank acquisition in my spare time and a few new loan origination offices we're trying to open. An office in D.C. should be open in sixty days, and Phoenix is ninety days out.

"Now for, the not so good." Nick leaned forward in one of the side chairs, hesitating a few seconds.

"As I said earlier, we're somewhat concerned about the examiners, who in turn are nervous about our ADC portfolio. The good news is that they're dealing data that's three months old, and generally, everything still looks fairly good.

"The bad news is that I'm starting to have some sleepless nights because of potential problems with a few of our borrowers or portions of our portfolio."

"Which ones?" Ron asked.

"Carr and Larson are a concern for a number of reasons. They're still current, but I'm not sure for how long. I'm also worried about Old Cyprus Country Club and our Texas portfolio, in general. Hideo's doing what he can, but I'm troubled by his lack of sales, both here and in Japan, and the oil problems are killing the regional economy in the Southwest."

Ron held up his hands.

"Wait a minute, Nick. Let's start with Carr and Larson first. What's the problem?"

"Several, but the first is that the tax-shelter market is continuing to dry up.

"We just ran out of interest reserves on a few of their deals that haven't been sold yet because syndication opportunities are moving slower than expected. The indication I'm getting from a number of sources is that the environment is going to get worse. I don't know when they'll get those sales closed.

"A lack of help from our congressional friends is killing, or at least putting off, any deals in process."

"It looks like our visits to Washington haven't helped much," Ron said.

"Well, the word now is that the changes shouldn't be as disastrous as originally proposed, but who knows?"

"Won't all changes in the law be prospective? I can't see why they'd make them retroactive," Bill said.

"I can't either, but I've seen stranger things happen when Congress and the IRS are involved."

"So continued sales of their finished product are nonexistent at this point?" Bill questioned.

"That's right."

"I thought these projects were viable with or without unusual tax breaks," Bill countered.

"They're supposed to be, but I don't know how much time and effort Stephen and Andrew have put into leasing and retaining. And frankly, we haven't analyzed the projects on any other basis."

"I don't understand. If they focused on leasing, they wouldn't need to flip the centers," Ron said.

"They have too many projects at the beginning stages to do that, and even more that have been on-line for a while and aren't where they need to be," Nick said, apologetically.

Ron hesitated, taking a deep breath.

"Why did we let this get out of hand? You're the chief lending officer—this is your responsibility."

"I know, I know," he stammered. A steady stream of perspiration was starting to run down his face.

Ron didn't speak, but his stare said everything.

"Another problem I see," Nick continued sheepishly, "is that several of their in-process centers are going to be in over-budget situations."

"This just gets better and better, doesn't it"?

Nick was silent.

"We have control of their construction money, don't we?" Ron asked, mechanically.

"Sure, but what do we do if there's not enough money in the loan to finish because of unforeseen costs or whatever? If we were dealing with class A developers or borrowers in this situation, they'd throw in a portion of their profits to help."

"Stephen and Andrew won't do that?"

"Hell no," Nick responded immediately. "They can't— they're too busy buying toys, like airplanes, helicopters, and yachts, or going on exotic vacations," He said, irritably. "They've already spent all the money they'll make for the next six months."

"And therefore, overdrawing their personal checking accounts," Lydia jumped in.

Ron quickly shot a glance in her direction.

"And do they make the checks good?" he asked.

"Eventually. This last go-around took two weeks to clean up. They gave us some bad checks to replace the originals, and we had to go back to them, but the third set was okay."

"I think their basic problem is that they're not taking care of business anymore," Nick said.

"What do you mean by that?" Ron asked.

Nick looked terrible. His eyes were bloodshot and his whole face appeared to be sagging.

"We all know that the only real control a developer or contractor has over spending is constantly being on the job and watching its progress and the subcontractors.

"I mean, those subs will steal you blind if you're not on them all the time; or they cut corners to complete the job quicker.

Nick stopped and looked at Ron, appearing to be waiting for a reaction.

Ron said nothing.

"If you're there often enough," Nick continued, "you can catch that type of thing, but if you're only on site periodically, you may have to rip apart or redo the work. That's expensive.

"And I don't think they're looking at the suppliers' invoices closely enough. I doubt if they care anymore about dotting all the i's and crossing all the t's."

Nick put his head down and rubbed his eyes, then looked up.

"I still think they build an attractive shopping center, but in today's market, you've got to do everything right to be a step ahead of your competition."

"So, what are we doing to rectify this, Nick?" Ron asked curtly.

Before Nick could respond, Ron continued.

"Part of our job, a big part, is to keep on top of our borrowers so this type of thing doesn't happen. We need this situation corrected!"

He hesitated momentarily and then continued calmly, "Is it necessary for me to intercede at this point?"

"My staff and I will take care of it," Nick answered, quietly.

"Fine. And have your people look at deals without any unusual tax benefits; strictly based upon a conservative multiple of the projected gross operating income."

Ron's eyes appeared to be glazed over, as if he was in a trance. Then he turned and looked at his CFO.

"Bill? Where are we?"

"The market is starting to falter a little. The reduction in our upward earnings trend hurt us, and the shorts and their stories don't help.

"We're pretty much out of any more potential to buy. All of us, including the board, have done what we can. Whether it's all we're permitted through the profit-sharing plan, or all we can individually buy with borrowings. Another push by the shorts would be a real test for our stock."

"How are the Fleshman's staying short so long?" Ron asked.

"We had them. I thought they had to deliver the borrowed stock in five days?"

"They're supposed to. I've got the NASDAQ Surveillance Department working on it. As soon as I find out anything I'll let you know."

Bill looked over at Nick. "Of course, the main reason for the stock's retreat is because we ran out of interest reserves on a few of our larger projects, significantly affecting the bottom line."

He hesitated. "It may be a good idea for some of my people to analyze the whole ADC area to see if we're headed down a one-way street."

"First of all," Nick yelled, his arm darting in Bill's direction, "your people don't know shit about lending! That's why we have analysts and compliance people in our department. They know what they're doing."

"They would have fooled me," Bill responded, quickly, locking Nick's gaze. "I sure as hell haven't seen any analyses or projections from them or you."

"Fuck you! I'll take care of the lending area."

Nick's body language dared Bill to question him again.

"Nick," Ron broke in, raising his tone an octave higher than Nick's, "Bill needs that information. Your people can continue to compile the data, but I want him to have copies of whatever they do."

"And I want a copy of the reports that you produce for the directors."

Nick's eyes became hostile.

"Listen, asshole..."

"Nick!" Ron interjected, "Bill uses that information as a basis for filing the regulatory reports, and the board members want someone outside the lending area to explain it to them. They told me that.

"He needs to know how all the numbers and classifications are put together. I want you to give him what he needs!"

"Lending is our area!" Nick shouted. "I don't want him involved."

"This is supposed to be a team effort, not a turf war," Ron yelled, his face flush.

"I can't believe your attitude. I don't want to hear any more of this 'my area, your area' shit. Is that understood?"

Nick hesitated, but finally nodded.

Ron was now visibly shaking. "We're done," he said.

"Nick, I want you to go over the Hideo Tabani scenario and your concerns about Texas with me the first thing Monday morning."

He got up, walked out of his office, and out the front door.

Jack stopped the car, jumped out, then ran around and opened the passenger door before Lydia knew what was happening.

"For my lady," He said, as he bowed and directed her into the car with his arm.

She smiled and took her seat, shifting slightly to get comfortable.

"So how was your day?" he asked as he slid in.

"Oh, it was okay, but I started to get a little anxious after you called and asked me to go to dinner with you tonight," She said, smiling.

"I couldn't keep my mind on my work. I really wanted to see you. Besides, it's Friday night. I'm sure you put in as challenging a week as I did. We need to unwind."

"So where are we going?" Lydia asked, as he pulled onto Military Trail.

He looked over at her, raised his eyebrows, and cocked his head to one side. "It's a surprise."

She faked a disappointed look.

"But, I guarantee you'll love it."

"Okay, I trust you—drive on."

Jack drove into Palm Beach on Royal Palm Way and down South County Road to Worth Avenue and the Esplanade. He had the car valet parked, and they walked up the stairs and into the Cafe L'Europe.

"I love these pink tablecloths and napkins," Lydia said, as the waiter showed them to a table in the corner. "And the way the restaurant is decorated overall. It's really beautiful."

"That's why I wanted to come here. It reminded me of you."

Lydia smiled, and started to blush.

The waiter came to the table, introduced himself and touched on the specials, leaving them with the menus and wine list.

"Would you like some wine?" he asked.

"I'd love some."

"Red or white?" Jack asked as he glanced at the wine list.

"Well, I think I'm going to have some fish tonight, so let's get some white."

He nodded, and then ordered a bottle of chardonnay. The waiter poured Jack a taste. He swirled the glass, checked for clarity, tested its nose, and tasted.

"Very good," He said, looking up at the waiter.

When both glasses were filled, he raised his.

"A toast to a great evening with a beautiful woman—how lucky can I be," He said, grinning.

She looked into his eyes and was intoxicated before her first taste of wine.

The sun shining through the hotel window awakened Lydia. She blinked her eyes as they adjusted to the light. Jack was just a few feet away in the king-size bed, staring and smiling at her.

"Good morning," He said.

"And to you."

The sliding glass doors were open, and a steady breeze was blowing the delicate white curtains back into the room.

"I know we're not at the Breakers, but it's near the beach," Jack said, apologetically.

"It's beautiful. Just being with you makes me very happy.

You know, it gets pretty hectic at Dawn, and I really don't have anyone I can talk to. Thanks for listening," Lydia said.

He ran his hand through her hair, and then kissed her gently.

"Anytime. I don't have any preconceived notions about anyone or anything at Dawn. Use me as a sounding board, if it makes you feel better."

She returned his kiss and he pulled her close.

Nick was sitting in a guest chair in Ron's office.

"Good morning," Ron said, as he walked in and hung his suit coat in the closet.

"Good morning," Nick mumbled.

"I know I was a testy yesterday, but I had every right to get upset. This ADC environment is extremely risky with the type of borrowers we have. All of us, and our people, are paid good salaries to keep on top of them, like stink on shit. Evidently, with Carr and Larson, we haven't done that."

Nick had his head down, avoiding any eye contact.

"Do you agree, Nick?"

"Agree with what?"

"That we haven't done all we need to do in lending oversight—especially with Carr and Larson."

"Yeah."

"And I certainly don't want to lend these guys any more money until we evaluate exactly where we are with each of their projects.

"For each center, you should address the interest reserve remaining, overall construction completion percentage, pre-signed leases, the lessee themselves, the total loan expected to be disbursed, and estimated sales price, with assumptions used. Any questions?"

Nick shook his head.

"Good. Now what's the problem with Hideo?" he asked, sitting down in the chair across from Nick.

"Well, the clubhouse is up, and we'll have the grand opening in a few weeks, but the sales just aren't coming."

"Does he have the course open for play?"

"Yes, and it's pretty steady, but only limited interest in homes or lots thus far. If that development was down here, it'd sell like hot cakes."

"But it's not, is it? It's in the middle of orange groves, way west of Vero, and we knew that."

Ron hesitated, stood up and walked to the window, looking out at nothing.

"It may take a little longer than we'd like," Nick said.

Ron turned around. "When is he going to open the restaurant?"

"Next week. He'll start with a daily lunch and dinner on weekends, and then expand, if it's appropriate."

"We're just going to have to watch the project closely. How much interest reserve do we have left?"

"Another four months.

"Ron, I really believe Hideo's trying to do all he can."

"I don't doubt that, but as I said before, all these deals are touch and go. We can't let any of them get away from us. I really feel that's what happened with Carr and Larson.

What about Texas?"

"We're about to run out of interest reserves on several of our projects, and I know there's more to come.

"Over and above the challenges we're having in Florida, the oil crisis is killing us in Texas. And related businesses are either slowing down considerably or closing their doors. Large sections of neighborhoods are being laid off or let go. The homeowners can't make their payments and are giving their keys back to their lenders."

"What about equity?"

"They bought their residences when everything was booming, and now their market values have plummeted. There's more debt on the homes than value, and naturally, the small shopping centers, warehouses and office parks are also dying."

"And that's where some of our borrowers are."

"That's right."

"I need an update on every project we've lent on. From this point forward, if you start to feel uncomfortable with any of borrowers or projects, I want to know early on, so I can get involved.

"If I wait until I get some of your regular reports, I could be months behind a problem."

"I understand."

ᕤ

"The information you got from your Florida connection was right on," Jake Fleshman said, as he walked toward his brother on the pool deck.

Larry's smile was almost too large for his face.

"Well, what should we do?" He asked, thinking out loud. "We're in the money now."

Without waiting for an answer, He said, "Let's buy back in and deliver, and then short again."

He put his arm around Jake. "I think this is going to be a nice ride, big brother. But this time, let's sell more. Let's sell everything Norton-Steele has in margined street name or whatever we can borrow."

"You feel that confident?" Jake asked.

Larry turned his brother around, holding both his shoulders. His eyes were on fire.

"Jake, my man. This is going to be a fucking blowout."

CHAPTER 11

"God," Bill said, as he walked into Ron's office. "The shorts are continuing to beat the shit out of our stock."

"They must have a hell of a war chest," Ron responded, continuing to look through the paperwork on his desk.

"I don't think there's any question, but I'm concerned about more than that."

Ron finally looked up. "What are you trying to say?"

"I think we have a mole. They know too much."

"Bullshit!" Ron responded quickly, obviously irritated and on edge.

"Maybe so, but I'm hearing things from brokers and analysts that mirror very closely conversations we've had in our management team meetings."

"For instance?" Ron asked.

"Well, we talked about being at the end of the line as far as our internal stock purchasing power, including our permissible pension fund acquisitions."

"They could have guessed that. What else?"

"That our delinquencies are a lot worse than the examiners think because they're looking at three-month-old data."

"You heard that, too?" Ron asked, closing his eyes and leaning back in his chair."

"This morning."

"So, I'm guessing that the regulators know that we're worse off."

"I would assume so."

"Any suspicions?" Ron asked.

"Not really. All of the members of the management team have a stake in this company—ownership, options, and a future."

Bill sat down on the couch and hesitated for a few seconds.

"You know I'm not crazy about Nick."

Ron nodded.

"But he loves this place—and you," Bill continued. "I don't believe he would do anything intentionally to hurt you or the company."

Ron massaged his eyes with his fingers.

"I'm glad you feel that way. I agree," He said, opening his eyes. "But I just don't understand how this information could possibly get out."

Bill could see the pain on Ron's face, but knew he couldn't do anything to help.

"I don't know either." He glanced at his watch. "I'm sorry, but I've got to run. It's Christopher's birthday, and I promised both he and Marie that I'd be home tonight for dinner."

"Oh sure, go ahead. You and I have both spent too many nights here," Ron said quietly, as Bill left.

"It's just so hard to fight and protect the company against people on the outside," he continued to no one. "But with insiders, it's close to impossible."

"Bill, if you don't mind, I want to stop at the Delray Office and see how it's progressing," Lydia said.

"No. That's fine. That Sun City grand opening was something."

He looked at Lydia, who was now grinning broadly.

"I thought Miami Beach was unbelievable, but Sun City was indescribable—the clowns and acrobats and other street entertainers. I thought I was on the Wharf in San Francisco!"

"I know. It was fantastic. And best of all, the customers loved it."

"And another million dollar day!"

Lydia scrunched up her face and smirked.

"Well, congratulations, my dear—you continue to outdo yourself."

"Thanks. I deserve the praise, but let's jump to another subject."

She held up her hand. "What are you going to do about attending Hideo's grand opening this Friday? Ron wants the complete senior staff to make an appearance."

"I really don't think I can make it, Lydia. I won't get back in town from my analysts' meeting in New York until six o'clock or so. By the time I get home, put on my tux, and drive almost two hours, it'll be over."

"First of all, it won't be over," She said, "but you would be late. Secondly, I talked to Ron about your time squeeze. He wants you to be there and suggested that we take the chopper."

"Oh please," Bill said, closing his eyes and shaking his head.

"Oh nothing. This is all company business, and we're doing it. Besides, it'll be fun. I'll bring Jack."

"You've been seeing quite a bit of him, haven't you?"

"I have," She said, her eyes sparkling. "He's really special."

"If you care for him, I'm sure he is."

Bill hesitated slightly. "You're right. We should be at the grand opening. The four of us will go in the chopper."

"Great," Lydia said.

❦

The helicopter landed in the empty lot next to the Casey house. Several neighborhood kids started to congregate.

Bill and Marie quickly finished getting ready, kissed Beth and Christopher, and gave a few final instructions to the babysitter. They rushed out, warned everyone not to get too close, and stepped into the rear of the cab. They greeted Lydia and Jack and sat down in one quick move.

Almost immediately, they took off. The kids covered their faces as the chopper threw off gusts of wind and scattered the loose sand and dirt as they made their ascent.

"Lydia tells me you were in New York," Jack said. "How was your trip?"

"Well, these analysts meetings are becoming more and more interesting," Bill responded. "We've got a couple short-sellers messing with our stock and peoples' minds, so it makes the presentations, especially the question and answer periods, more challenging. But we're getting by."

"Good. I know it must be difficult," Jack said.

"It is, but Bill's up to it," Lydia said, patting him on the arm.

"I understand you brought us the Old Cyprus deal," Bill said.

Jack nodded, smiling.

"We've all heard that it's beautiful," Marie added.

"Thanks, it is. And Hideo is a hard-working developer. I believe we're blessed to have him here," Jack said.

They continued their flight to Vero, not far over the treetops, trying to identify some of the landmarks they were passing as the evening was starting to settle in.

The helicopter started to slow down somewhat.

"I guess we're here. It's hard to tell in the twilight," Bill said, as he looked at the surrounding area.

"There's the clubhouse." He pointed.

"It's really lit up," Jack commented.

"Well, the sides of the building are almost all windows, and the skylights are a nice touch. Hideo wanted to bring the outside in, taking advantage of the gorgeous views," Bill said.

The pilot made a quick, smooth descent. Everyone on the porch was watching the helicopter, waiting to see who the passengers were. As it landed, the pilot stepped out stooping under the blades, opened one side of the cab, and then ran around to open the other door.

As Bill got out of the helicopter, he looked up, and all eyes were on them.

"Lydia," he yelled, trying to be heard over the noise. "I guess you can't arrive unnoticed when you travel this way."

She looked back, grinning. "That's okay. I appreciate this few minutes of notoriety."

She walked ahead and up the stairs with Jack, with an aristocratic gait befitting her entrance.

❦

"Hideo, this is a fantastic grand opening party," Lydia said, as she looked around the crowd of people. "Everyone's having such a good time."

"I understand from what Ron and Nick have told me, that coming from you, that's quite a compliment."

"Yes, it is," She said, laughing.

"We call her Ms. Modesty, Hideo," Bill interjected, looking around. "Are Ron and Nick here yet?"

"Oh, yes. They came early."

"Hey, where did Marie and Jack go?"

Hideo surveyed the room. "They're talking with Stewart Bell and Yasuo Kitamura. Ron and Sara are with them."

"Who did you mention first?" Lydia asked.

"The two golf course architects," Bill responded.

"Now I remember."

"Can I get either of you another drink?" Bill asked. "I'm going over to get myself one."

"Why don't you wait a few minutes?" Hideo asked. "The grand entrance for our touring golf and tennis professionals is just about to begin."

He nodded to one of his people on the other side of the room. Then Hideo looked back at Lydia and Bill.

"Of course," He said, smiling, "it won't be as grand as your entrance, but it will be nice."

As the three were laughing, they could hear Vivaldi's *The Four Seasons* being played, first slightly muted, then somewhat louder. The music was coming from an area at the edge of the dance floor that was surrounded by large plants, behind which, stood a railing.

First heads appeared, and then the full form of an ensemble of musicians.

In the forefront, stood three tuxedoed gentlemen, two holding golf clubs and one with a tennis racquet, all appearing magically with the assistance of a rising floor.

The crowd applauded and Hideo beamed. He walked forward, opened a small gate, entered and picked up a microphone.

"Ladies and gentlemen. I again welcome you to the Old Cyprus Country Club. We are very happy that you could join us this evening, celebrating what we hope will be a very successful golf and tennis residential community.

"I especially wish to thank Ron Jameson and Nick Donofrio from Dawn Savings. Without their faith and support, we would not be here this evening. Please join me in thanking them."

"I didn't know he was going to do that," Ron said, looking at Sara and the Donofrios during the applause.

"But it's nice, isn't it?" Sara said.

Both Ron and Nick nodded, acknowledging the thank you.

"I'd also like to introduce you to Art Conroy, our tennis pro and Kiichi Soko and Fred Nelson, our golfing professionals.

"As you probably know, Mr. Conroy won several tournaments last year, both here and abroad, and is currently ranked number five in the world.

"And both Mr. Soko and Mr. Nelson have been consistent money winners all over the globe.

"Please join me in making them feel at home," He said, leading the audience in an applause.

"Now please," he continued, "introduce yourself to these gentlemen, and maybe arrange an outing or lesson.

"We'll be here tonight for several hours, so have something more to drink, and feel free to dance to the music of Spectrum. As their name suggests, they play anything.

"Thank you, again," He said, as he put the microphone down, and then stopped, bowing to more applause.

※

"That slant-eyed son-of-a-bitch. Look at him smiling. He's got Jameson wrapped around his little finger," Andrew Larson said, sneering from a corner on the other side of the room.

Stephen Carr quickly looked at his partner, appearing shocked. "What in the hell are you talking about? And who are you to slur Hideo."

"I'll tell you who I am. I'm part of a team that hasn't

been treated properly by its bankers. They should be falling all over us for our business.

"Instead, they're all over us because of a few bad checks and some development setbacks. And that Jap's treated like a king."

"First of all, keep your voice down," Stephen said, looking around the room. "And secondly, I think you've had too much to drink. I'm leaving now, so if you want a ride back to the house, I suggest you leave also." He started to walk through the crowd.

"Fine—I'll go," Andrew mumbled. "But my days of being pushed around and not treated the way I should be are over."

"Good morning, Ron," Lydia said, as she walked into his office.

The *Wall Street Journal* was open, and he was staring, giving no response.

She put her hand on his shoulder, squeezing slightly.

"Ron."

He turned his head. His eyes were bloodshot and somewhat glassy.

"I'm sorry, Lydia, did you say something?"

"Yes, but I was speaking softly," she lied.

"I just couldn't sleep last night," He said.

Ron shook his head and then turned toward Lydia, repeating what Bill had told him the previous day.

She sat down and listened with great interest, not believing what she was hearing. After a while, it appeared that she was no longer listening.

"Are you okay, Lydia? You don't look well."

She took a deep breath and forced a smile.

"No, I'm not, Ron. I feel weak all of a sudden. I'd better go home early."

"Sure," He said, getting up and walking her to a chair. "Can I help you?"

"No," She said. "I'll be fine."

"You should sit down for a few minutes," Ron said.

"No, I can't. I have to go."

She got up and walked toward the door.

"Hope you feel better, Lydia."

"Thanks," she responded, as she left the office.

Lydia picked up the telephone in her office and dialed.

"Jack."

"Lydia, what a nice surprise."

She took a deep breath to gain her composure.

"Can you meet me in a half hour at our spot by the ocean?"

"Sure. Any special reason?"

"No. I just want to see you."

"I'm looking forward to it already."

Lydia hung up the telephone and stood there for a few minutes motionless.

❧

Jack was waiting. The sky was clear and blue. The ocean was relatively calm, with the movement of the waves against the shore, gentle and very peaceful.

She walked to him. He opened his arms, smiled and closed his eyes.

"You bastard!" Lydia yelled.

She put her whole body into her right arm and slapped the side of his head, knocking him to the ground.

He lay there, not quite certain what happened.

"What's wrong?"

"What's wrong? You lowlife," she yelled louder.

Tears and mascara were streaming down her face.

"How could you betray my confidence?"

Jack propped himself up on his elbow, using his other hand to shade the sun from his eyes so he could see his aggressor more clearly.

"I don't know what you're talking about, Lydia."

That comment evoked new terror. She kicked his arm, and he fell back.

"How can you lie to me?" She pleaded, having expended all of the energy she had within her.

"Lydia, I can explain."

She walked away from him, sobbing uncontrollably, sitting on the first of many benches that lined the beach.

He got up, walked over and sat next to her, putting his arm around her shoulder.

The rage returned. Her eyes were like lasers as she shook off his arm.

"Don't touch me. Don't come anywhere near me!" She said, as she turned away from him.

He stood up.

"At least give me a chance to explain."

There was no response.

"You know that Barbara and I have been separated for years. We have a lot of debts. She spends on herself and the kids like there's no tomorrow. I needed money to get out from under. Then when you came along, that became even more important."

She looked back.

"So you used me," she cried, her eyes filling with tears, but her voice remained strong.

"For us, Lydia, for us," he interrupted before she could continue.

Lydia started to breathe slower, allowing her brain rather than her emotions control her body.

"You have no idea what you've done," She said, shaking her head in disbelief.

"I trusted you, I...I loved you, if that's possible."

"Lydia, I..."

"Don't—it's too late."

He looked away from her gaze.

"Ron Jameson and Dawn Savings helped me get through a terrible time in my life. Ron and that company mean everything to me. And you're in the process of trying to destroy both. I don't believe your shallowness."

Jack's eyes were moist, and his shoulders were drooping.

"I'm sorry, Lydia—I never meant to hurt you."

She looked directly into his eyes. "If you ever cared for me, Jack, don't come around me again. Please, leave me now."

She looked away toward the ocean, her tears and trembling returning.

After a few minutes, she turned slightly and saw him walking toward his car. She started to breathe slowly, matching the ocean's rhythm.

"I am so ashamed of myself," She said to no one. "How am I going to tell Ron?"

It was 3:30 a.m. and the telephone rang. Bill instinctively grabbed the receiver and lifted it to his ear.

"Hello?" He said, half-asleep.

"Bill. I need to talk."

"Lydia, is that you?"

"Yeah. Can we talk for a few minutes at *Mom's*?"

"Now," He said, hesitating—still trying to get his bearings.

"Do you know what time it is? He asked, as he glanced at the clock."

"I do, but I really need your help."

"Okay. I'll be there in twenty minutes," He said.

It was always breakfast at *Mom's*, but the local eatery was quiet at close to 4 a.m.; Just one coffee-drinking couple that looked like they had been out for a night on the town and had found a refuge to regroup.

Bill saw Lydia in a corner booth. She had her back to the front of the restaurant. The lights were muted during the early morning hours, but he recognized her silhouette as she fidgeted nervously.

He walked to the booth and glided into the open seat, simultaneously looking across the table at his friend.

She looked bad. Her hair was anything but combed, and her mascara was all over the bridge of her cheeks. But it was much more than that—he could tell from deep within her eyes. He had no idea where the pain was coming from. He put his hands over hers in the center of the table.

"What's going on?"

"I don't know where to start," She said.

"Any where you want," He said, forcing a smile.

"I really trusted Jack, and I told him a lot of things I shouldn't have."

"Like what?"

"I let him know about my frustrations with Nick, and the stupid things he was doing. I needed someone to talk to."

"So what? It's no big deal. Jack seems like an understanding person. I'm sure he knew you needed to vent and that your conversations were confidential."

"No," Lydia said, looking away from his eyes.

"What do you mean, no?"

"I mean no," She said, pulling her hands away from his and rubbing her eyes.

She looked back up at Bill.

"Jack passed on what I told him to the short-sellers. I was the leak through him."

Bill shook his head. "You've always used me as a sounding board when you had problems with Nick. Why did you have to talk to an outsider?"

"I didn't feel it was fair. You had the same problems with Nick, and you couldn't talk to anyone else other than Marie. I know she didn't want you to make the move to Dawn in the first place, so she probably wasn't your best listener, and I didn't want to dump anymore on you than you already had."

Bill took a deep breath, looking at Lydia with no expression.

Her tears started to fall.

"I had no idea," She said. "You've got to believe me."

Bill hesitated, and then held her hands.

She couldn't look at him. The tears were still flowing.

"I believe you Lydia. That's not where I'm having the problem. It's with Jack. He's not the kind of asshole we need right now."

"I know. I feel like such a fool. This whole situation is eating Ron up, and I can't even imagine how I'm going to tell him. I've really let him down."

"Listen. There's nothing you can do about the past now. Ron's a fair person, and he cares for you. Be honest with him. That's all you can do."

❧

The telephone rang.

"Jack Graham."

"It's Larry. I haven't heard from you in a few days, and we need to stir up the market. What's going on?"

"Nothing's going on. My cover's been blown."

"How?"

"Lydia figured it out. Too many things she told me were out on the street. She's a smart lady."

"You care for her, don't you?"

"My feelings for her aren't really relevant here," Jack said, irritably.

"I'll do what I can to see this thing through, just as I promised, but I no longer have any value in the role I was playing."

❧

"Can I see you for a few minutes?" Lydia asked, as she stood in Ron's doorway.

Even though her appearance was as impeccable as ever, she looked worn out and the whites of her eyes had a reddish cast.

"Sure...sure," He replied.

He got up out of his chair and walked over to her.

"I know you weren't feeling up to par yesterday. You still look a little tired this morning. Are you okay?"

Her eyes started to moisten, and her lip began to quiver as she looked into his eyes.

"Come on. Let's sit down."

He put his arm around Lydia's shoulder and escorted her to the couch. They sat, and she took several deep breaths.

"You and Sara were wonderful to me during the most difficult time of my life," She said.

"Being nice is easy with you."

"I don't know if that's true anymore," She said, her voice starting to crack.

"Why do you say that?"

"I'm the mole!" she blurted out.

"The what?"

"The mole. I'm the person that passed that damaging information on to the short-sellers."

His smile vanished, and he adjusted himself on the couch.

"Please explain, Lydia. I'm confused."

Lydia continued. "Okay," She said, looking down at the floor. "You know that I really cared for Jack."

He hesitated when she used the past tense.

"And him for you," Ron said. "It's been pretty obvious."

"It could have all been a show on his part."

"Pardon me?"

"I'm not sure how much of his affection was real and how much was artificial."

"Why?"

Lydia explained the passing of information between Jack and Larry Fleshmen.

Ron didn't respond.

"Believe me, Ron, I didn't know what he was doing. I thought I was in love and I trusted him. I felt comfortable talking with him. I had no idea he had other motives."

"How did you find out?"

"I guessed. No one else on the management team would have betrayed you or the company. A light went on yesterday when you told me some of the things the brokers and analysts evidently knew. They were all things I discussed with Jack."

"So that's where you went after you left here—to talk with him?"

She nodded. "He had money problems, and this was supposedly his way out."

Ron was expressionless.

She stood up. "It's over with Jack and me, and what I did was a terrible thing. I realize that it won't make the situation any better, but I feel I must resign." Her voice was quivering.

Ron pursed his lips. "You're right—it was terrible—an unforgivable breach of trust."

Her body started to shake visibly and the tears flowed.

Ron stood up and held her.

"Jack violated all of us, but you not only trusted him, you loved him, and he deceived you. I know how that must hurt."

She pulled back slightly; her eyes were filling with tears.

"Are you trying to tell me that it's okay if I stay?"

"That's what I want. This organization couldn't function without you."

"But, Ron, how can you trust me?"

He put his hands on her shoulders and held her firmly.

"You made a mistake in judgment. It's over. Now you need to get back up on the horse and ride."

He walked back to his desk and sat down.

"Lydia, we've got a lot to do to get us out of this hole. We'd better get busy."

"I'm really pleased that you're finally getting the reports that are distributed at our loan committee meetings, Bill," Alan Adamson said.

"So am I."

"Frankly, when I ask questions," he continued, "I really

don't get answers that I understand. And when I continue to ask for clarification, Nick gives me the impression that I shouldn't be concerned. 'That's why you hired us,' he says. As the Chairman of the audit committee, I don't like it."

"Neither do I," commented Arnie Cohen.

"You did the right thing," Bill said. "My asking always gets me into a struggle with the lending people. You talked to Ron, and I got my first earlier today. And I'm also on the distribution list for all future copies. Thanks."

"Thank you. You give us straight answers," Alan said.

"Okay then. Any questions from this morning's loan committee?"

"Yeah," Adamson responded quickly. "The delinquency report."

"Okay."

"The first column is 'Gross Delinquent Payments'. Then there's a column called 'CIT' that's subtracted from the gross numbers to arrive at 'Net Delinquent Payments'. Evidently, one of those numbers is reported to the regulator. Is that correct?"

"Well, we report delinquent loans, but I'm not sure which of the numbers the lending group gives us. Before now, I didn't even know there were two.

"Doug Carson or one of his people in the special loans department completes the delinquency information and then sends the total over to accounting to be included in our regulatory filing."

"Can you find out for us whether it's gross or net and what the difference is?" Adamson asked.

"Sure. I'll go through the proper channels and get the answers for all of us."

"We don't want to be pains in the ass, Bill, but that CIT number keeps getting bigger. As of today's report, it's two million," Cohen added.

"Listen, guys, anytime you have a question, it's your job to ask, and ours to get you an answer."

"Okay," Adamson said. "Let's start reviewing these large invoices. We've got quite a few this month."

"Do me a favor and hold any questions that you have on the invoices. I'll be back in less than an hour."

Bill walked down the hallway to the special loans department, and through the open doorway. The staff was on phones or busy with correspondence. He nodded and waved as he walked through the offices. Doug Carson was sitting at his desk, going through some paperwork.

"Doug, how are you today?" Bill asked, as he sat down in one of the guest chairs.

"Not bad," Carson responded, putting the papers neatly aside.

"We're busy, and in this department, that's not good, I guess. On the other hand, personally, I'm fine. What can I do for you?"

"Well, as you know, you just started to copy me on your delinquency report."

Carson nodded.

"I received the first one this morning. A few members of the audit committee are meeting as we speak, and since I was with them earlier, they asked me a few questions I couldn't answer. For their benefit and mine, I thought I'd stop down and get some answers while they're doing some of their other work."

"Fire away."

Bill looked at the report he had carried with him.

"As you know, there's a gross column, and a net column. The difference is something called CIT. What is that?"

"That's collections-in-transit."

"Collections-in-transit. Can you define that for me?"

"Sure." Doug straightened himself up in his chair.

"As you know, we talk to these people as infrequently as once a month, or as often as a couple of times a week, depending on what we think is appropriate."

"I understand that."

"Well, I call or visit our larger borrowers.

"Based upon those conversations, if I feel the payments that are delinquent will be received within the next couple of weeks, I consider them to be collections-in-transit."

Bill pulled his chair closer to the desk.

"So this column doesn't represent checks in your possession that just haven't been deposited by month-end?"

"No. The 'Gross' column would have been adjusted for that."

Bill sat back in his chair. He looked at Doug intently. "Who told you to use the 'CIT column?'"

In a relatively nonchalant manner, Doug answered, "No one. I felt it was appropriate."

Bill leaned forward. "Appropriate for what? So we're in deeper shit than we already are with the regulators?" Bill said, curtly. "How long have you been doing this?"

Doug's face was beginning to flush. "The last several months—five or six maybe, but in the beginning, the numbers were small.

Listen, you're going to have to talk to Nick if you have a problem with my reporting. He never questioned what I was doing."

Bill stood up, looking down at Doug. "You're a lawyer, for God's sake, and you've had experience in collections. What you're doing is not only wrong—it's fraud.

The examiners and auditors haven't been here since you started using CIT; otherwise you and Dawn would be nailed to the cross." Bill's expression was intense, his eyes glaring.

"I know you understand that your numbers are sent to the regulators every month. Which ones do you give the accounting department for the reporting, net or gross?"

"Net," he answered quietly, looking away from Bill's glare.

"I don't want to discuss this anymore. Talk to my supervisor."

"That's exactly where I'm going."

Chapter 12

Bill went directly to see Nick Donofrio and walked past his secretary.

Nick was going over some project plans that were laid across his worktable in the corner of his office. His back was to the door.

"Can I have a few minutes of your time?"

Without turning Nick said, "I'm busy right now."

"This is important, Nick. We need to talk."

"Fine," He said, flopping down on the couch. "What do you want?"

Bill looked down at him. "I don't want to be here any more than you want me here," He said, irritated at Nick's attitude.

"I asked you what you wanted."

"You know I got my first delinquency report today."

"Yeah. I wonder who put that bug up the audit committee's ass."

Ron walked in and smiled. "It's nice to see you guys working together," He said facetiously. "What's going on?"

Ron sat at the other end of the couch.

Bill, feeling more relaxed, sat down in one of the guest chairs.

"I was just about to tell Nick that I appreciated receiving my first set of loan committee reports."

Nick glared at Bill, but said nothing.

"While I was meeting with the audit committee they asked me what the 'CIT' column was. It's used as a subtraction item from gross, to arrive at net delinquencies.

And that net number is included in the reports we file with the regulators."

"And?" Ron said.

"As you both know, it's up to two million dollars. They were concerned because they didn't understand what it represented. They said that it's been climbing the last several months. Since I was interested myself, I went to visit Doug."

He looked at Nick. "Do you know what collections-in-transit is?"

"Checks received, but not yet deposited in the bank," He said, without hesitating.

"Wrong."

"What do you mean, wrong?" Nick asked

"Yeah. What do you mean wrong?" Ron echoed.

"CIT are 'feelings' about getting payments. It's not even the infamous 'the check is in the mail.'"

"That's bullshit!" Nick said, standing up.

"That's exactly what Doug told me. And believe me, I went over it several times to make sure he understood what I was asking.

"When I questioned him on its' appropriateness, He said that he felt that approach was reasonable."

"I don't believe it!" Nick said, sarcastically.

"Go talk to your department head."

"I agree, Nick," Ron said. "Go talk to Doug and find out what's going on. It's the last day of the month. We'll be filing another report in ten days or so. I want it to be correct."

"I'm sorry, guys. I can't give you an answer on the CIT yet," Bill said, as he walked into the boardroom.

"That's all right. We really didn't expect it today," Adamson said.

"Are you okay? You don't look good."

Bill glanced down, forcing a smile. "I'm fine. Let's go over your questions on the invoices. We don't have much time," he continued. "The day's almost over."

✌

Cathy Demming tapped on Bill's door. "Good morning," She said, opening the door slightly

"Good morning," he responded, looking up from his work.

"Sylvia called. Ron wants to see you in his office."

"Okay," He said.

Bill stood up and walked past her, through the executive reception area, and into Ron's office.

Nick was already there.

"So what did you find out from Doug yesterday?" Ron asked.

Nick looked only at Ron, not Bill.

"Evidently, what Bill told us yesterday was correct. And most of the adjustments were made to the Carr and Larson credits."

"So that means that our real delinquency situation is even worse than we had thought."

"That's right," Nick said quietly.

Ron leaned back in his seat and shook his head.

"How could he just make adjustments to numbers based upon his expectations?" Ron asked.

Nick raised his arms up. "I don't know."

"This guy is dangerous," Bill commented.

Nick turned to Bill. "He made a mistake."

"A mistake? Yeah, a big fucking mistake! That decision,

he evidently made on his own, without any guidance from you, was completely illogical. He's a professional. He should know better."

"Maybe so, but I should have caught it, and I didn't," Nick countered.

"I'm not trying to fix blame," Ron said. "I just want it corrected."

"It's done. I told him that I didn't want any more of those adjustments. Actual payments received are all we're going to consider in the future."

Sylvia walked in the room. "Ron, your eleven o'clock is here."

"Fine. We just finished up here. Give me five minutes, and then send them in."

Bill stood up, putting his hand on his forehead.

"Wait a minute! This asshole just commits fraud, so we slap him on the hand, and it's over."

Bill looked over at Ron. "I want to talk to you privately."

Nick almost jumped up, standing in front of Bill. "I told you it was a mistake."

"Get out of my face," Bill responded, his eyes glaring.

Nick stood his ground.

"Move, Nick," Ron said, "and then get out of my office."

Ron looked at Bill. "Sit down," he said.

"I don't feel like sitting down," Bill said, walking toward the window, his back to Ron.

"What's on your mind?"

Bill turned around abruptly. "What's on my mind? The same thing that should be on your mind: Nick! He's the disease that's going to kill this place—if we're not already dead."

"Don't you think you may be giving up too soon?"

"Giving up? I'm not giving up. I'm telling you that this organization cannot survive with Nick here. Because he was with Dawn from the beginning with you doesn't mean anything to me. All I see is what he's done since I've been here—and it's not pretty."

"Nick's a smart guy, and I want to stick with him for awhile longer. If I'm wrong, I'll handle it at the appropriate time."

Both men were silent for several seconds.

"Okay, Ron," Bill said, turning to leave. "You're the president, and it's your call—but the appropriate time may have already past."

The telephone rang.

"It's Doug. We're in deep shit. They found out."

"What about Nick?" Andrew asked. "Can't he help?"

"I think he's starting to catch on himself. We were only able to get this far because he doesn't like to mess with the details. He left that to me."

"So now he knows the details?"

"Yeah, I think so. I think he realizes that we're working together—he's not stupid, just naive."

"What happened?"

"The numbers were getting too big. Casey and a few of the board members started to ask questions he couldn't answer." Doug hesitated. "I never liked Casey," he continued.

"He's an asshole," Andrew said, "and he'll soon learn not to mess with us.

"But he's small potatoes. Jameson's the real problem. He likes to be the big shot, doling out money to his friends."

"I don't know—I've never had a problem with Ron. I think..."

Andrew yelled loud enough to cause Doug to move the telephone away from his ear.

"I said Jameson is the fucking problem!" as he slammed the telephone down on the receiver.

Bill was standing in Kathryn Baker's office in the accounting department, bringing her up to date on the CIT scenario.

"I don't believe it," Kathryn said, a disgusted expression on her face. "How could he make that kind of decision on his own?"

"I don't know if he did. Nick seemed surprised, but at the meeting this morning, he didn't have a whole lot to say. On the other hand, Doug told me that he thought the adjustments were appropriate."

"I don't want them to just give us numbers anymore. Now that I get the delinquent reports, we can complete the filing with the regulators ourselves."

"By the way," She said, "this could be a coincidence, but we got some fairly large checks from Carr and Larson late yesterday afternoon. Stephen brought them in personally and gave them to Doug."

"So he brought them in on the last day of the month. Has he been doing that right along?"

"Not lately. They were bouncing quite a few checks for a while, and then they stopped making payments."

"Well, I know their leasing and syndication sales program has slowed down," Bill said.

He hesitated for a few seconds. "It's still an unbelievable coincidence that when they stopped paying, Doug started adjusting their delinquency amounts."

"It sure is."

"I feel uncomfortable about this whole situation. I'm going to send you a memo explaining that any checks we receive at month-end that subsequently bounce should be reversed as far as the previous month's work is concerned.

"So all reports, both internal and external, will be affected.

I'll copy Doug and the senior staff."

The telephone rang.

"Bill, it's Kathryn. Guess what?"

"I don't know. What?"

"It's the fifth of the month, and all the Carr and Larson checks bounced."

"Surprise, surprise. Did you adjust all our reports?"

"Not yet, but I will. Should I redeposit?"

"Sure, but don't wait to reverse the transactions. The chance of them having any money, or any they want to give us, is slim.

"Oh, I've got some news for you," Bill said, coyly.

"Go ahead.?"

"Doug Carson resigned. You know where he's going?"

"I know this is kind of wild, but how about with Carr and Larson?"

"Did you ever consider becoming a mind reader on a part-time basis—in the evenings and on weekends, maybe?"

"Are you serious? I was right?"

Before he could respond, Kathryn continued

"That slime ball."

"You took the words right out of my mouth. I've got to run."

"Bill."

"Yeah."

"I'm afraid of what else we're going to find."

"You and me both."

❧

"So what did you want to see me about?" Ron asked Nick, "the regulators?" as he walked into his office and sat down.

"No. They're still not done with their work."

"When will we get the results?" Ron asked.

"They'll probably contact you directly in a few weeks."

"Then what can I do for you?"

"Carr and Larson came to see me this morning. They've made an offer on the Post estate in Palm Beach," Nick said quietly, looking away.

"The Post estate? On South Ocean Boulevard?" Ron asked, shifting in his chair. "How much do they want?"

"The purchase price is six million. They need five and a half million from us. They put up a two hundred thousand dollar non-refundable deposit in escrow as earnest money."

"What did you tell them?" Ron asked quietly.

"I explained that I would have to discuss the situation with you."

Ron's eyes widened. "Why in the hell did you tell them that?"

Nick looked at Ron, as if looking for sympathy.

"Well, they're our best customers. I felt we owed them at least a discussion."

Ron twisted in his chair.

"First of all, they are by no means our best customers. Unfortunately, they're our biggest customers. Secondly, we can't even get them to pay us on future income-generating projects. How do we get them to pay us on a personal residence?"

Before Nick could respond, Ron continued.

"And what if we have to take it back? What's our chance of selling a fucking six million dollar white elephant?"

"I thought..."

Ron stood up. "Nick, you're exasperating me."

He started to pace around the office.

"You started to say that you thought, but that's your problem, you don't think. I don't know what's going on, but I want you off the Carr and Larson projects. For the time being, your staff and I will assume responsibility for their relationship."

"But, Ron..."

"Nick," Ron said.

He walked over, putting his hand on Nick's shoulder. "You're all stressed out, and you're starting to make me that way. You need a break, man."

"I know, but there's so much to do."

"Look, I'm temporarily taking away what appears to be one of your major problems. You keep telling me what a great staff you have—let them earn their salaries. Take a few weeks off, and then jump on everything else you have to do. And don't forget the regulators—they can kill us. Do you understand?"

"Yes, sir."

CHAPTER 13

"I don't give a fuck what your policy is! We're your biggest customers, and your policy should be designed for us!" Andrew Larson yelled through the speakerphone.

"You and Stephen are certainly our most significant borrowers, and that's all the more reason for us to make sure that our underwriting on your individual loans, and frankly on the complete relationship, is thorough and on-going.

"Besides, as you know, Andrew, several of your credits with us are delinquent. I really don't know what our loan committee is going to say about your tentative purchase of the Post estate at his time," Ron responded. "I wouldn't be very optimistic at this point."

"The regulators are watching us very closely until we can reduce our delinquencies," added Bill Casey, who had been sitting with Ron when Larson called.

"We've got two hundred thousand God-damned dollars on the line!" he barked. "And I don't really care about your regulatory difficulties or your internal policies. We didn't have this problem when we dealt with Nick."

"Well, you should have spoken to us before you put up that kind of money.

"We're your lender. This is not an account that you can draw from whenever you feel like it. Every transaction has to be evaluated on its own merits—and you're no longer dealing with Nick. I'm working on your projects.

"Besides, as I said, this is a completely new ball game, and we're not managing alone anymore. The regulators are in the dugout with us."

"Listen, Jameson, we want our money, and we want it now! I'm getting tired of our company putting out all the work and effort, and then having assholes like you and your team control our destiny."

"This conversation is over, Andrew. None of us need to be verbally abused by you or anyone else."

"It'll be more than verbal if we don't get what we want."

Jameson was quiet for a few seconds, and then asked in a slow and deliberate fashion, "Are you threatening us?"

"You interpret my comments any way you like, but I'd recommend that you, your people, and your families be careful. There are a lot of weirdoes around."

"Where's Stephen?"

"He's in Sweden, completing the financing arrangements with the government for our new yacht because you shitheads wouldn't do it," Andrew said, sarcastically.

"You guys never stop, do you?" Ron said.

Andrew's yell made the speaker phone crackle. "We're only getting what we deserve! Nobody's going to stop us!"

The telephone was thrown on the cradle, and Andrew was gone.

"He's one sick puppy," Bill said.

"All drugged up," Ron interjected. "I don't think there's a chemical out there that he's not using for something."

Stephen's a very good businessman, and I know Andrew sees that. I really believe he thinks that everyone looks at him as Stephen's sex object."

"Do they?"

"Sure. I mean the guy is very intelligent, but he has an extremely low level of self-esteem. Unfortunately, he ends up going to the opposite end of the spectrum to overcome that feeling about himself and acts like a real asshole."

Ron hesitated.

"Like most of us, his personality is almost a direct result of his upbringing."

"I don't know anything about him."

"Well, Stephen gave me a little history on Andrew when we were talking one afternoon. It's a long story, but here's a recap.

"He was born and raised in Jamaica, but came to the U.S. as a high school exchange student and never went back. His grandfather was an English transplant, and his father is a very successful businessman on the island.

"Evidently, his father was tough on him—a religious zealot. He's constantly trying to prove himself and at the same time, rebel. Unfortunately, he doesn't have the confidence to make it on his own. He's very unstable."

"That may be the understatement of the year," Bill responded. "Do you think he was serious about his threats?"

"Do you want to take the risk that he's bluffing? I mean, the chances of the loan committee giving those guys any more money are nil. I'm sure as hell not going to recommend it. We have too many of their problems already."

"So what are you going to do?"

"I'm not sure yet, but I know we need to take some kind of protective measures. I'm going to talk to the executive committee tomorrow."

"Yeah?"

"Larry Fleshman?" Andrew asked, aggressively.

"That's right. Who is this?" Larry answered, defensively.

"Who this is isn't important right now—it's what I know that's significant."

"For example?"

"I know that the delinquency reports Dawn Savings has been distributing internally and filing with the regulator have been falsified."

"That's significant. The regulators and the market would probably be very interested in that information."

"You bet your ass."

"So what's in this for you, Mr. Incognito?"

"That's my business. When I have more, I'll call you."

Before he could respond, Larry heard the dial tone.

"You're not serious. He really threatened you?" asked Alan Adamson.

"Bill was there with me. We couldn't believe it."

The committee members started talking among themselves; their feelings fell somewhere between shock and disbelief.

"Unfortunately, Andrew is an extremely unstable individual. Considering the state he's in now, I wouldn't put anything past him."

"How much have we lent these people?" asked Neal Sparkman.

"Over fifty million dollars," Ron said, quietly.

"Over fifty million! How could we have been so stupid?"

Ron answered calmly, "Neal, we don't make bad loans to questionable people. Carr and Larson are class B or C borrowers. We don't get the A's. That's who we deal with, and we all know that.

"On the other hand, they've been successful at building and syndicating shopping centers. Changes in the tax law and some construction delays have thrown off their operation, and as you know, they're delinquent on some of their loans.

"Larson doesn't seem to be able to cope well. That's something we were unaware of."

"I'm telling you, those people are all messed up mentally."

"What people?" Ron asked.

"Queers," Neal fired back. "It's not natural. They don't think like us."

"I'm not interested in their sexual preferences, but only whether they can pay back their loans," Ron stated.

"Neal," Adamson jumped in, "we all ratified the loan committee's decisions on their projects.

"We've also all been invited to attend their committee meetings, so we could hear the detailed explanations of the projects. I think Ron and the rest of our lending team have been very open with us."

"I know, Alan. I'm just frustrated. The tail seems to be wagging the fucking dog at this point, and I don't like it.

"Our family has been in business in this area for forty-five years, and we have a very good reputation. A major problem here could ruin everything we've built."

The room was cold with air-conditioning. Neal had his suit coat off, but his shirt was wet with perspiration.

Ron eyes were clear and unwavering as he looked at Neal.

"As far as our portfolio is concerned, we're naturally concentrating our efforts on working out all of our problem loans, including these. However, that's not the reason I updated you on the Carr and Larson relationship."

"I don't understand," Neal responded.

"Considering the state Andrew is in, I wouldn't put anything past him. And as I said, he's threatened the senior staff and our families."

"What do you recommend, Ron?" Adamson asked.

"I recommend that we have security systems installed in all the senior officers' homes and cars.

"Here at the office, a guard will replace our receptionist, and cameras will be installed around the perimeter of our building.

"I've already taken the liberty of asking a consultant who specializes in executive kidnappings to put on a seminar for all officers. Even without our current problem, this is not unusual for a large corporation.

"On their own, several of our people have applied for gun licenses."

"You're not serious?" Neal said.

"What would you do if you and your family were threatened? I'm not interested in carrying a pistol, but I can't blame those of my people who do."

"Well, I agree that we shouldn't condone carrying weapons, but certainly we should do everything in our power to protect our people and their families," Adamson said. "We've always told our employees that we care, and this is a perfect opportunity to show them that's the case."

As Adamson spoke, Neal was nodding in agreement.

"Ron, we're with you all the way. I don't think anyone on the board will question your suggestions. I just hope they're all for naught."

"Only time will tell," Ron said.

Stephen tried to unlock the front door, but realized that it had been left open. He walked into the hallway and stood at the bottom of the spiral staircase.

"Andrew," he called. "Andrew."

There was no response. He picked up an empty Jack Daniel's bottle from the floor and put it into the basket in the kitchen.

Stephen noticed Andrew's pillbox lying on the sink. It was usually filled with a mixture of goodies from a pharmacist friend. He typically kept it close at hand, but now there was no need—it was empty.

Stephen glanced out of the sliding glass doors and noticed Andrew sitting on the pier, looking out over the water. He slid the doors open, walked out, and stood next to his lover.

"I need your help," Stephen said.

Andrew looked up. He was wearing dark sunglasses.

"Help doing what?" he asked slowly.

Stephen sat down on the pier, looking at Andrew and shook his head.

"You're really blasted. It's one o'clock in the afternoon, and you have no idea where you're at."

"I know where I'm at," Andrew said defensively.

Stephen took a deep breath and looked out over the Intercoastal, trying to force himself to relax.

"Andrew, we're going to lose everything if we don't lease up the property we've got."

He turned to Stephen, "Jameson's shut us down—he's killed us."

"It's not a big deal—only a temporary stoppage. The more income we can generate from our centers we already have, the more valuable they become. The more valuable they become, the wealthier we are. Comprendez, amigo?"

Andrew smiled. "The eternal optimist."

Stephen put his arm around his companion and squeezed.

"Let's go get some lunch."

Chapter 14

"Ron wants the senior staff in his office for a meeting," Sylvia said, as she moved through the executive area.

Bill stepped out of his office. "Now?" he asked.

"Immediately."

Lydia, Bill, and Nick hurried into Ron's office. He looked tense and pensive.

"So what's up?" Lydia asked as she sat down.

"We're in deep shit," he responded with a serious expression. "I know we tried to do the best job possible when the examiners were here, but our effort wasn't good enough."

"Damn it! I knew they wouldn't let up. They've got it in for us," Nick said.

He jumped out of his seat, not letting Ron continue. His face became beet red.

"Those shitheads have never worked in a financial institution and wouldn't know one if it bit them in the ass.

"And worse yet, most of their crew are just out of school. What the hell kinds of conclusions are they going to reach?"

"Nick," Ron called, but Nick continued to wander and talk.

"Nick!" he called again, much louder.

"Sit down and let me finish!"

As Nick sat, Ron continued.

"As you no doubt remember, when the regulators were here the last time, their main complaint was our lack of proper loan documentation and control. Our argument was that our loans were substantially current, and that was the 'proof of the pudding.'

"Well, with our current delinquencies, we no longer have an argument. We were supposed to clean up our policies and procedures."

"So we hired Albert Hurst & Company and they put together a beautiful manual," Nick interjected.

"That's right, but we haven't been following it," Ron continued.

"The regulators are very close to making us sign a relatively onerous supervisory agreement, restricting our commercial lending. I don't know if we can stop them."

"That's bullshit!" Nick yelled, standing up again and strutting around the room. "We just got them out of here—they can't do that."

"Damn it, sit down, Nick!" Ron yelled. "They sure can. They can do almost anything they feel is appropriate."

"Maybe this action will be good for us," he continued. "Hopefully, now we'll concentrate on correcting our documentation and underwriting problems instead of continuing to push garbage out of this company."

Ron hesitated, taking a few deep breaths, glancing at his senior staff.

"The meeting's over," He said.

"Nick, stick around. I want to talk to you for a few minutes."

As Bill and Lydia filed out of the office, Ron began. "Nick, we've got problems. I..."

Nick interrupted, obviously nervous, but not conceding, "Ron, we've done everything they've asked for."

"No, we haven't!" Ron countered.

"We were all warned after the last exam that we had these holes in our operation, and I asked you to correct them," Ron said, pointing his finger at his chief lending officer.

"For God's sake, Nick, it's been over six months since we were warned the first time."

"I know," Nick responded meekly. "But we've been so busy. Look at the tremendous profits our group has generated."

Ron shook his head and then looked at Nick.

"Where the hell have you been? Our profits are dropping like a lead balloon. Most of our credits were substandard from the outset."

"Well, that's true of the old loans, but what about the new loans we've put on the books?"

Ron put his hands over his face, massaging his eyes. Without moving his hands, he spoke very slowly.

"Nick, you're a very intelligent person. You know as well as I, that the most substantial reason our new loans are current is the interest reserves that we've built into those loans.

"Our older borrowers have generally depleted theirs, and since their sales have been slow and their personal equity is tight, they haven't been able to make payments.

"When you deal with B, C, and D borrowers in a tough real estate market, negative things happen. However, some of these loans should never have been made."

Nick was quiet.

"You're too interested in pleasing the borrower and developing relationships. You're not analyzing the proposed transactions like you should. In this business, that's just not following the regulations, that's not using good business judgment."

He took his hands off his eyes and looked at Nick across the desk.

"Maybe this is a good time to evaluate your career," He said, hesitating, "and determine if this is what you really want to be doing."

Nick looked at Ron in an almost childlike fashion, his eyes drained of his typical enthusiasm.

"But the financial industry and Dawn are a major part of my life. What else would I do?"

"I don't know, but you need a change. You're moving in too many different directions without completing any one. You're drifting, Nick, and leaving a lot of damage in the process."

Nick sat down without a response.

"Listen," Ron said, "I'm telling you this as your friend. You need to get out of this business. Not necessarily today, or tomorrow. We're still putting commercial loans on our books, and I need your help with the Arizona acquisition. Just keep your eyes open, for your own good."

Nick appeared to be in a state of shock, staring for a few minutes.

"I've got a lot of work to do," Ron said. "I'll discuss this with you more over the next several weeks, if you'd like."

Andrew continued using drugs and alcohol in greater and greater quantities, and his and Stephen's relationship became increasingly strained. Andrew was starting to spend most of his time in the guest bedroom at the rear of the house by himself. Stephen intentionally stayed away, hoping to give his lover some space and an opportunity to get his head together. However, he was starting to worry. It had been several days, and he had not seen Andrew.

He came home from a meeting with his leasing agent, and again, Andrew was not around. He walked down the hallway and knocked on the door to the guest bedroom at the rear of the house. No answer. He knocked again. No answer. He opened the door and walked in.

The room was dark, with all the shades drawn, but there were white candles burning everywhere. A heavy incense was in the air, and he heard an eerie form of music, with chimes and instruments he didn't recognize. The total effect made him feel uneasy.

He could barely make out Andrew at the far end of the room. He heard him speaking to someone, but no one appeared to be with him.

"By thy power, Master of Crossroads, Papa Legba, remove the barrier for me, so I may pass through and speak with the other 'loas'; I need their help. When I come back, I will salute you, loa Voodo Legba."

There was approximately thirty seconds of silence, and he started to speak again.

"Your magic will be complete, serpent god Nickballahwedo, and you have given me these drugs to protect me. My enemies cannot hurt me now with their magic."

"Andrew. Andrew!"

No answer.

As he walked farther into the room, Andrew became more visible and Stephen noticed that he was sitting in a lotus position, his back very erect and completely focused. He evidently had no idea that anyone was there. Stephen noticed a short table in the far right corner with a large black cross, crowned with a bowler hat and clad in a frock-like cloak. A long table lay just ahead of Andrew, strewn with a number of burning candles, playing cards, cocaine dust, a snorting straw, and what appeared to be five small dolls.

Stephen had known Andrew was mildly interested in voodoo from his boyhood in Jamaica, but he had discounted his comments about the practice as "typical" Andrew—out in left field. He surveyed the room. Andrew's formerly mild interest was now out of control.

Stephen picked up one of the dolls, and then each of the others, one by one, looking at each head. They were effigies that resembled Ron Jameson, Bill Casey, and several loan officers at Dawn. Each had at least a dozen pins inserted through the body.

"I don't believe this. What in hell are you doing to yourself?" He grabbed Andrew by the shoulder. "What is this shit?"

Andrew appeared to be incoherent.

"I said, what is all this stuff?"

"It's exactly what you see," Andrew answered slowly, looking up at Stephen.

"Ron and the rest of Dawn are responsible for our problems, and I'm making them pay. They feel the pain, Stephen! Believe me, they feel the pain!"

"Let me tell you something, Andrew. They don't feel anything, and you're killing yourself! You're using too much of this stuff," he yelled, looking down at the cocaine dust.

Stephen shoved everything off the table and stormed out of the room, slamming the door.

Bill left the *Taboo* restaurant in Palm Beach after a dinner meeting with Ron. It was 10:00 p.m. and drizzling slightly. He was walking quickly to his car north of Worth Avenue. The side streets were almost deserted.

A man wearing a hat and an all-weather coat was jogging in his direction on the sidewalk, but Bill paid him no particular attention. It was raining and those people that were out were looking for cover.

As the stranger reached Bill, he turned quickly and shoved him into an alleyway, where another man threw him against the rear wall of an apartment building, kneeing him in the groin. Bill fell to the ground in pain, curling up in a fetal position.

One of the aggressors pushed his hand on the side of Bill's head, forcing it against round drainage stones. He tried to twist to see his assailant, but the hand made that impossible.

"My wallet's in my pants. Take it and leave me alone," He said unemotionally, still stinging with pain.

The man holding his head eased the pressure on his hand and then immediately grabbed Bill by the hair and lifted his head from the ground slightly, staying slightly to the side and rear.

"Listen, Casey, I don't know who you are and don't care. But I understand that you keep throwing around Andrew Larson's name in vain. He doesn't like it, and therefore we don't like it. This is just a warning—keep it up and we may have to visit you again."

The stranger smashed Bill's left temple into the stones. "The next time, we won't be so nice."

Bill waited five minutes or so before he got up. His head and groin ached. He felt dizzy.

Andrew Larson, he thought. *The only place he ever speaks about Larson is the management team meetings, and Nick's his asshole buddy.* Bill shook his head, trying to rid himself of the implication for now, and it hurt. *They could have killed me if they wanted to,* he thought. *They won't come back tonight.*

He slowly walked to the car and drove to West Palm Beach.

I can't tell Marie about this. It's just another part of a bad story that's getting worse.

❧

He opened and closed the front door quietly, knowing the kids were sleeping.

"Hey, big guy," Marie said, as she came around the corner from the family room. "How was your dinner with Ron?"

Before he could answer, she looked closer at him, then put her arm on his. "Bill, you don't look good. Are you okay?"

"Oh yeah, I'm fine," he lied. "I just..."

"Look at your pants — they're ripped," She said, kneeling down to get a closer look. "And you're bleeding."

Bill tried not to show his surprise. His adrenaline was running, and he didn't even feel the cut knee until she mentioned it.

She stood up and looked into his eyes. "Bill, what happened?"

He bent over and looked at his knee.

"I think I may have had too many glasses of wine with Ron," He said, looking back up at her.

"I really didn't want to admit that, but as I was walking to the car, it was wet, and I slipped on a curb. My footing wasn't very good, and I went down like a rock. But you know," He continued, looking down at his pants. "I didn't even realize that I ripped these."

She looked into his eyes and asked, "Are you telling me the truth?"

He put his arms around her waist and pulled her close.

"Why would I lie to the most important person in my life?"

❧

Bill left the following morning with Ron on a two-day road show for analysts, brokers, and institutional investors in New York. There was no mention of the incident from the night before.

The environment in New York was becoming more and more difficult. The rumor mill was out of control, fed directly or indirectly by the Fleshmans. But Ron had a calming affect on the audience.

As soon as he spoke, the market for Dawn stabilized after weeks of gyrations. Bill wondered how long the players would feel as strongly about his supervisor and friend.

They arrived home Friday night, and Saturday morning Bill walked into the Dawn Corporate Offices at 10:00 a.m.

The building was quiet, except for a muffled conversation going on behind Nick's door. He opened it without knocking.

Nick was sitting in a Queen Anne's side chair talking on the telephone. The first expression Bill read as their eyes met was that of fear. That was all he needed.

Nick stood up. Without hesitating, Bill hit his former friend on the edge of his nose and base of the right eye with such force that he knocked him and the chair onto the floor.

Before he could react, Bill leaped over the chair, jumped on Nick's fallen body and wrapped his hand around the front of his neck, squeezing. The color washed from his face. Blood was running down the back of Bill's hand from Nick's nose.

"I can't breathe—let me go," Nick pleaded in a high—pitched, hardly audible voice.

"Listen, asshole," Bill responded, his eyes unwavering and cold. "Your friend, Andrew almost had me killed the other night. Do you really think I give a shit whether you can breathe?"

"I don't know what you talking about," Nick argued as Bill's grip became tighter.

"You've been talking to Andrew Larson about private conversations the management team had, and evidently he doesn't like how I feel about him."

"I didn't know."

"It doesn't matter whether you knew. You're a cancer to this organization."

Nick tried to get up, resisting Bill's hold on him, but he couldn't budge.

"Dawn is my life—I've given everything I have to this company."

Bill's expression became even more intense. He bent over Nick, almost nose to nose.

"What you've given Dawn has been a waste. All you care about is yourself. Because of you, this wonderful organization is dying. Get out now, before you destroy everything positive about this company."

Bill took several deep breaths, slowly let up on his grip, then stood and walked out the door.

"Mr. Carr is here to see you," Sylvia said over the intercom.

"Fine. Send him in, and get Bill."

"Ron, how are you?" Stephen said, as he walked in and shook Ron's hand. His demeanor wasn't as friendly as the salutation.

"I'm fine. And you?"

"As well as can be expected. I'm still upset about your not financing the Post estate transaction. I hope you realize that you threw away two hundred thousand dollars of your own money," He said, sarcastically.

"You mean your money."

Stephen held up his hand as if to cut off the direction of the conversation.

"Believe me," He said, "bottom line—it was yours."

Bill walked into the room.

"We were just talking about his purchase of the Post estate," Ron said.

"You mean, the purchase that fell through at great expense to Dawn," Stephen said.

Ron ignored the comment and continued. "Please sit down, gentlemen. Did you get your financing in Sweden for the yacht?" he asked, looking over at Stephen.

"You knew I was there?"

"Andrew told us."

"Sure. You're not the only lender that will finance us. They didn't give me the final okay, but I have the feeling we'll get a positive nod."

"Well, you may have to do more of that."

"What do you mean?"

"Borrowing from elsewhere. The regulators are all over us.

"Because of the size of your relationship with Dawn, you and Andrew are a large part of their conversations and restrictions. Your loans are all substantially delinquent, and I understand you've got another large negative balance in your checking account.

How much is that overdraft, Bill?"

"It was approximately two million dollars as of yesterday's close."

Stephen abruptly stood up. He looked down at Bill, his face tightening.

"That accounting department of yours is all fucked up! This has happened before, and..."

"That's right, Stephen, it has happened before," Ron interrupted, "and they were right, just as they are now. You're overdrawn two million dollars. And the games are over.

"We've bent over backwards to accommodate you and Andrew, probably too far, and now we're in deep shit."

"You didn't do us any favors. This relationship was good for you too," Stephen said sarcastically. "And by the way, it's Dawn that's in trouble, not us."

Ron stood up, walking toward Stephen.

"Is that right?" He asked, looking up at his aggressor, but stopping only inches from his frame.

"What are you going to do for income when the regulators refuse to allow us to finish funding your projects and demand that we throw them into foreclosure?"

"They can't do that!"

"You watch them. And I say 'them,' because I won't be here anymore—they'll be running the show."

"I'll bankrupt the companies. They're each in single-purpose subsidiaries, and the regulators won't be able to touch me personally. It'll take them years to get the properties."

"You're not getting the message," Ron said, his face getting tighter and flushed.

"Do you think they care how long it takes? This is a bureaucracy we're dealing with! In the meantime, you're paying your lawyers for a lost cause, paying real estate taxes, unless you want the county to take the properties, and generating no income. No rents, no sales, no nothing. They'll go to court and get 'stays' on everything."

Stephen said nothing.

"Listen to what I'm telling you," Ron continued. "This is the end for all of us unless we can clean up this mess."

Stephen walked over to the couch and sat down.

"And how do you propose we do that? You know what the market is like, and I'm having problems with some of my subcontractors."

"And," Bill added, "you and Andrew are spending money like water."

Stephen leaned forward, pointing his finger at Bill.

"No one tells Andrew and me how we have to spend our personal funds."

Bill stood up and walked to the couch, looking down at Stephen.

"How do you figure it's your personal money when you're two million dollars overdrawn?"

Ron walked over from the window, standing between the two men.

"Guys, we've got to get together on this, or we're going nowhere," He said calmly.

Stephen put his head down, and then he looked up at Ron.

"We don't have any money. How can we bring ourselves up to date?"

Ron sat down. "You've got one asset that's not delinquent."

"World on the Bay," Stephen said proudly.

"Exactly, and it's been appraised for substantially more than you paid for it."

"And the value will skyrocket when we convert it," He said with a smile, the first since he walked in the office. But it only lasted a few seconds.

"So where are you going with this conversation?"

"We want to buy it from you."

"For how much?"

"Twenty million, which is the appraised value of the property. That'll be enough to pay off your mortgage, clear up your overdraft, and bring your other loans to no more than thirty days past due."

Stephen said nothing immediately, then he stood up, looking at Ron and Bill.

"Fuck you both! Andrew was right. You're only out for yourself."

He started to leave, and Ron walked over to the door.

"This is for all of us, including you and Andrew. They're going to shut us down, Stephen, and this is the only way you and Dawn even have a slim chance at survival."

Stephen stopped, and then walked over to the window, staring for a few minutes. He turned around and looked at Ron.

"We'll want a buy-back option. I know that place can be a gold mine."

"That's no problem. You can buy it back for exactly the price we pay you for it, plus closing costs."

"Fine," Stephen grunted.

"How are you going to convince Andrew? The last time we talked to him, he was wild and crazy. He threatened all of us and our families."

"He's having some problems that he needs to work out. Those drugs are finally starting to affect his mind. I'm trying to get him off the stuff, but before I do, I'll get him to sign whatever needs to be executed."

"That's the right thing to do, Stephen," Ron said with a tired smile.

"I've got to go.

I know you're in a box, but I'm still not happy about this," He said, as he walked out of the room.

Bill put his arm around Ron's shoulder. "Good job. I didn't think you could do it."

"Thanks. I guess I won that round, but I don't feel like it.

"Get the guys from Latham Parish to complete the documentation as quickly as possible. Let's get it done before he changes his mind."

"You got it."

"Next is Hideo. This is going to be even tougher. He's truly a nice guy," Ron said under his breath.

"See you tomorrow," Bill said, walking out the door.

"Sure," Ron answered, half-heartedly.

John Richmond, Director of the Federal Home Loan Bank's Atlanta office just hung up the telephone. He received another anonymous call about Dawn Savings. This one warned of more serious loan problems than his staff had reported during the last examination.

The caller also mentioned fraud and that congress wouldn't be happy with any regulator that was soft on the industry. Too many high flyers were taking advantage of the system on the backs of the American people. The elections were around the corner, and the politicians wanted blood.

"Ron, Nick's here to see you."

"Thanks, Sylvia, send him in."

Nick walked in and sat down. His nose was covered, but it didn't completely hide what appeared to be a major black and blue section of his face, or his bloodshot eye.

"What in the hell happened? Sylvia said you were sick, but I thought it was the flu?"

"Quirk accident at home—no big deal," He said quickly, cutting off further conversation.

"Fine," Ron said, not appearing to believe the response. "So, what's going on?"

"Well, I've got a couple things I'd like to talk with you about."

"Go on."

"I know you've been able to work out a temporary fix with Carr and Larson, but our problems in Texas have gotten a lot worse."

"I'm aware of that. Our guys are doing the best they can down there. Unfortunately, it's going to be a long-term effort.

What else, Nick? What's on your mind?" Ron asked, irritably.

"I talked with Bill this morning. He just finished working with our numbers for February. Quite a few of our ADC loans in Florida are or will be delinquent in the next few months unless our borrowers sell a bunch of units or lease a ton of space. I don't believe that's possible in the current environment."

Ron pulled his chair closer to his desk.

"Overall, considering our total portfolio, what kind of delinquency percentage are you talking about?"

Nick hesitated for a few seconds. "Eighty-five percent, or so."

Ron pushed back slightly from his desk, stroking his chin and staring out the window.

"I knew this was coming," He said, not really talking to Nick, even though he was there.

"It was inevitable. All the indications were there over the last six to eight months. Florida and Texas were over-built. Nothing was moving. Most of our large borrowers didn't have enough equity in their deals to take them seriously. It was only a matter of time."

He looked back over at Nick. "What else?"

"I was able to get a position with Les Greene. I'll be leaving in four weeks."

Ron hesitated slightly. "Good—he's a successful developer," he commented, with little enthusiasm.

"What will you be doing for him?"

"I'll be his financial person. He still has three more phases to complete up on the coast, and several other projects in the pipeline. He needs financing, so I'll start to visit some of our competition."

Ron nodded his head. "Anything else?" he asked, again with no emotion.

"No. I guess that's it," Nick said, getting up.

Ron stood up and shook hands with Nick.

"Congratulations," He said, looking away. "I'll send out a memo announcing your resignation and new position this afternoon."

"Thanks." Nick said, looking uncomfortable. "I'll give you several replacement recommendations by the end of the week."

"That won't be necessary. I'll be assuming that role, and Bill's assisting me," Ron replied, already seated and looking at some of the correspondence on his desk.

"But, Ron, Bill doesn't..."

Ron looked up with a cold stare.

"It's over, you've resigned—leave it alone. Please close the door on your way out."

Ron didn't wait for a response, but put his head down and continued his work.

Chapter 15

Bill and Ron were driving north on the interstate toward Vero and were almost at the exit. Ron had said very little on the trip, hardly responding to Bill's comments or questions.

"I think you're wrong on this one," Bill said, looking at Ron.

"What do you mean, I'm wrong?" Ron asked.

"Do you think I want to do this? He's almost out of reserves, and the loan is ready to become one of our largest single delinquencies."

"I know you're down on Nick's decisions right now—and that's understandable—so am I. But I believe he was right on this one, and that we should do everything in our power to keep Cypress alive.

"I've thought a great deal about this credit, and I really believe that it's only timing. It'll go—it's just when."

Ron didn't respond as he turned off at the Vero exit and headed west.

"Hideo's very close to signing an agreement with the sister club in Japan he's been talking about. Actually, he's dealing with Taiheiyo Club, Inc., an owner and operator of several properties over there."

Ron continued driving, his eyes focused on the highway, saying nothing.

"Do you know what they pay in Japan for a membership to a club?"

Before Ron could answer, Bill continued.

"At some of the better clubs, over a half million

dollars! Here they can get a house or a condo besides the membership and have money left over."

"He's still too far from Vero," Ron said. "And he doesn't have a beach available to him."

Ron looked directly at Bill. "What are the three most important things to remember in real estate?"

"I know. Location, location, and location," he responded. "But look at this road. There's development-in-process almost all the way out. And he's also about to reach an agreement with the Vero Beach Club."

"The reciprocity he was talking about?"

"That's right. Things are moving, Ron."

"For God's sake, there's no time," He said, looking at Bill.

"Have I ever been hesitant about foreclosure or taking deeds-in-lieu?"

"No. So why now?" Ron asked, sharply.

"What are we going to do with this place? Run it ourselves, or hire a contractor who doesn't really give a shit? And how successful will we be?

"Maybe it is too far away from Vero, but we're already here.

"Hideo has his life and soul in this project, and we trust him.

"Who feels more strongly about its' success? He's the best man for the job. Better than you and me, and anyone else we try to find, and you know it."

Ron was silent.

They drove past the unmanned guard gates, along the winding road between the eleventh and the twelfth fairways, and up to the clubhouse.

It is beautiful, they both thought independently.

A parking attendant took their car, and they walked up the few steps to the restaurant.

Bill looked around the room. There were about a dozen people dining—not bad, for a relatively new club at midweek. Hideo was visiting with some of the diners, but came over as soon as he noticed them.

"Gentlemen, I'm so pleased that you came to visit me and this beautiful facility."

I'm sure this guy knows why we're here, and he's still as courteous as the first day I met him, Bill thought.

"And we never tire of seeing our friend," Ron said.

Hideo smiled. "Now you're starting to sound Japanese."

"Coming from you, that's a compliment, indeed. Shall we sit and talk?"

"Certainly, my table in the corner has been set for us," Hideo said, leading the way.

"There was quite a bit of play on the course as we drove in," Bill said

"Yes, but the fees just won't be able to save me, will they?"

He sat down, his lips forming a smile.

The three men were quiet for a short time—Ron was staring at the course, and then he turned to Hideo.

"We've decided to give you a few more months," he said, taking a deep breath.

Bill looked at Ron, who appeared relaxed and nonchalant.

"I've heard many rumors and read newspaper articles concerning Dawn Savings. It must be difficult for you," Hideo said.

"We're having some very challenging problems," Ron responded with a tired smile, "and therefore we can't lend you any more money. But we feel so strongly about you and this project, and your ability to make the sales you need over the next several months, that we will continue to take the risk."

"I don't quite understand, Ron," Hideo replied. "If nothing has changed, then why did you come out here today?"

He waited for a moment and then continued speaking.

"Bill sounded uneasy when he called me to set up this meeting."

Ron put his arm around Bill and smiled.

"He has a lot on his mind. I've got him working in several areas, and he was probably preoccupied when he talked to you.

"You've got to stop that, amigo," Ron said, as he squeezed Bill's shoulder.

He looked back at Hideo.

"We came out here to tell you that no matter what you've seen on television or read in the paper, we're going to continue to support you as long as we can.

"Unfortunately, we don't know what that time frame will be."

"A few months are all I need."

"Hopefully, we'll all get a few months.

"We have to get back to Boca," Ron continued.

"I'll walk with you outside."

The attendant ran to get the car.

"I expected this day to be one of the worst days of my life," Hideo said, with moistened eyes. "Instead, it has turned out to be one of the best."

Ron patted Hideo on the shoulder.

"Good luck, my friend," He said, as he tipped the attendant and got into his car.

Ron glanced over and Bill was looking at him, smiling.

"Don't say it," Ron said.

"Say what? I was just going to comment on the weather.

"What a day," Bill added, looking out the window. "We should have brought our clubs."

❧

"Gentlemen, I asked you to attend this special board meeting for a couple of reasons. First of all, as a few of you already know, Nick Donofrio has resigned," Ron Jameson began.

"Why did he leave, and where is he going?" Neal Sparkman asked.

"We challenge each other a great deal here at Dawn—not everyone can live in a pressure cooker and still lead a relatively normal life. Nick felt it was time to move on."

"Since he was our chief lending officer, the state of our portfolio probably helped him arrive at his decision," Sparkman added.

"It was probably a factor," Ron said.

"To answer your second question, he's going to work for Les Greene, one of the developers we do business with."

"But you are ultimately responsible for this loan mess," Neal continued.

"Yes, I am," Ron responded, his eyes locking with Neal's.

"When's he leaving?" asked Ed Marks, interrupting the intensity.

"He's already gone. He gave me four weeks notice, but I suggested that he spend some time with his family and get his life in order before he starts with Les."

"What's your feeling as far as replacing him?"

"I don't believe we need to replace him. As we all know, our company has significant difficulties that we have to work out, and I need to get closer to them.

"More expansion, potential mergers, etc., will wait until we get our act together.

"In the meantime, I've asked Bill Casey to assist me with the portfolio. He's good with numbers and with people."

"I agree," Alan Adamson commented.

"In fact, he's already helped me start the restructuring of the Carr and Larson relationship. We'll spend more time discussing exactly what we're proposing at our next loan committee meeting."

Ron shifted in his chair.

"The second reason I asked you here today is because a representative from the Federal Home Loan Bank of Atlanta wants to meet with us next month."

"Why?" Adamson questioned.

"I'm really not sure. We still have net worth, so they can't close us down. But the reserves we've set up over the last several quarters and our current operating losses are eating away at us fairly rapidly.

"And since the results of the exam they've just finished may not have been good, they'll probably ask us to sign a supervisory agreement with some heavy duty restrictions, with the possibly that we'll no longer be permitted to make commercial loans or worse."

"I don't understand," Adamson commented. "I thought we were making positive strides with the underwriting process."

"Well—not as much of an improvement as I'd like. Plus they may be concentrating on our past underwriting problems and on the current state of our portfolio. It could be a lot of things."

"Based on what I'm hearing, you probably didn't object to Nick's resignation?" Sparkman asked.

"Like I said, not everyone is fit for this type of business environment."

"Over and above our own internal shortcomings, I've read several articles in the paper pointing out the pressure Congress is putting on the Federal Home Loan Bank Board to get tougher," Ed Marks commented.

"Sure—the hot button is to rein in troubled financial institutions. Unfortunately, as far as they're concerned, we're in that category."

He looked around the room. Everyone appeared to be listening intently.

"But that's really moot. The important point is that we are where we are, and they want to meet with us.

"I believe their restrictions could be significant," he continued, "significant enough to put us out of business completely. And if that's what they want, you should know what the alternatives are before you sign anything.

"If we're doing what we feel is right, we may not want to acquiesce to the regulators.

"As you know, Terry McCormack, from Latham Parish, is with us today. He's worked on several projects for us and has spent quite a bit of time studying the situation we're in currently.

"Terry," Ron said, looking across the table, "why don't you give us your conclusion."

Terry nodded.

"To quickly summarize my findings, I believe that there may be adequate legal support for us to refuse to sign any document forced upon us by the Regulators. In fact, we may have the basis to sue the government for harassment if they continue to pursue us unjustly."

"What do you mean by 'may be adequate legal support'?" Sparkman asked. "Is there any precedent?"

"Not direct, but indirect."

"This doesn't sound good to me," Sparkman said.

"I didn't say it would be clean or easy. However, we have a staff back in Philadelphia that's ready to start the war, if appropriate."

"But you've done the research, and you and Latham Parish feel that we should fight any significant restrictions?" Adamson questioned, looking at Terry.

"That's right."

"Are the senior staff members supposed to add their feelings at this point?" Bill asked, looking at Ron.

"That's why you're here. Jump in if you have an opinion."

"I believe that if we refuse and sue the government for harassment, the only winner will be Latham Parish," Bill said, looking around the table at each participant.

"I agree that we don't want to have our hands tied. Our underwriting policies are now being used properly, and we're starting to make better loans. But there's no question that some justification exists for every criticism they have. We have a tremendous number of problems we have to work out."

"But don't you need time?" Terry asked, his voice growing louder.

"It won't work," Bill replied. "Every time we try to sell or restructure an asset, they'll request a stay from the courts and hold it up. We'll get nowhere."

"So you want to roll over," Terry continued, smirking.

Bill was getting irritated at Terry's choice of words.

"I think we should fix what we can fix and try to work with the regulators as long as we can," Bill said. "They don't want to take this company if they don't have to."

"That's enough guys," Ron intervened, raising his hand.

"I'm just doing what I was asked," Terry said.

Ron closed his eyes momentarily, and then continued.

"I would like you all to take the work that Terry's prepared and read it over the next few weeks. He has a copy for each of you.

"Please call and tell me what your position is, so we're ready when we walk into that meeting.

"Any questions?"

"Will Terry be available so we can speak to him directly?" Adamson asked.

"He'll be in Philadelphia, but you can call him and ask any questions you'd like. He will also be in our offices the day before the meeting, just in case there are any last minute concerns."

"But you feel that the worst that will come out of this meeting is a supervisory agreement?" Adamson asked.

Ron nervously played with his mustache, and then took a deep breath.

"Honestly, I have no idea."

There were no smiles at the meeting being held at the Hyatt. The Federal Home Loan Bank of Atlanta and the Office of Examinations and Supervision requested the board sign an agreement, thereby putting the company under onerous restrictions and guidelines, over and above the standard regulations of the industry.

The board and loan committee were left intact, but for all practical purposes, in name only. Decisions of any significance were required to be ratified by the regulators before execution.

John Richmond, the regulatory representative at the meeting, had explained the seriousness of Dawn's financial condition, and the additional constraints under which Dawn would be placed. He also mentioned that the board's refusal to execute could be risky for them personally.

Any resolve on the part of the board to stand firm against significant restrictions was short-lived.

As they were passing the document around the table, Richmond continued to speak.

"One more thing. We want Ron Jameson's resignation."

Until that time, most of the people in the room were relatively quiet.

Ron looked at each member of the board, but said nothing.

"Is that really necessary?" Adamson finally asked.

Before Richmond could respond, Sparkman, who was sitting across from Adamson, moved as close to the table as possible. His face turned crimson, and he yelled, "You continue to defend him? Don't you realize what he's done to us? He's ruined our name in the community, and our stock is almost worthless."

He quickly turned his head to look at Ron, his eyes intense.

"He deserves everything he gets and more!"

"Gentlemen," Richmond interceded, "the answer is that we're not demanding anything at this time, but I would strongly advise you to sign the agreement and accept Mr. Jameson's resignation."

"If we do what you suggest, will we be sued by the government?" Arnie Cohen asked.

"Mr. Cohen, I'm not with the Office of General Counsel. That's their decision.

Besides, this is still your company, and you have a certain amount of liability as board members. I would recommend that you discuss any exposure you feel you have at Dawn with your own legal counsel."

With that comment, Richmond passed a prepared resignation to Jameson. Ron's face was expressionless, as he again looked at each of the directors. No one spoke or met his gaze.

He quickly scanned the document and signed.

"I must ask you to leave, Mr. Jameson. Please do not go back to your office or to the company's headquarters at all, for that matter.

Your personal belongings will be boxed up, and you will be called when you can come and get them.

In addition, I would like the keys to your company car. You will have to find your own way home.

Any questions?"

"No."

Jameson's hand calmly went into his pocket, pulled out his keys and handed them to Richmond.

The sky was deep blue, and the white cumulus clouds were so perfectly formed that they almost appeared artificial. But picturesque surroundings were of no significance as Ron left the Hyatt.

He walked to the curb and nodded at the doorman, who immediately called him a cab. Ron handed him a dollar bill as he opened the door.

"Boca, please."

The cabby headed south on Interstate 95. "Nice day, huh?"

"No. Actually, it's been fairly shitty."

"What?"

Ron ran his hands through his hair.

"Look," He said, taking a deep breath and calmly continuing, "this has been a disastrous day for me, and I'd rather just stare out the window, if you don't mind."

"No problem. I've had a few of those myself," He said, as he turned on the radio and drove south on Interstate 95.

✌

Richmond looked around the table.

"I would like to excuse the senior officers at this time."

Lydia Lewis and Bill Casey quietly got up and left the room.

"Gentlemen, since Ron Jameson has resigned, the company needs a new chairman and president."

"Well, what kind of latitude do we have here?" Cohen asked. "I guess I'm not sure where we're at."

"I'm not either," Adamson added.

Several of the board members nodded in agreement.

Richmond hesitated.

"Dawn Savings still has some net worth. Granted, it's well below required levels and you're losing money on a daily basis, but you do have some capital as we speak. If you extrapolate, the company has four or five months of equity left."

"So what does that mean?" Adamson asked.

"Well, your most important task should be to raise more capital as an independent organization, if that's possible, or try to sell or merge yourself."

"What about our ongoing losses? How do we stop those?" Sparkman asked.

"I really can't tell you that. The locomotive may be moving down the track a little too fast to stop at this point, but I believe you should try.

"Your remaining staff has a great deal of expertise in this business, and they haven't given us any reason to be concerned about the way they operate. That's why they're still here.

"If I were you, I would probably rely on them, and possibly supplement with someone who has experience in the workout area. You can try and hire a new CEO, but considering the short-term nature of the company, it might be a futile effort."

"So what's your alternative?" Cohen asked.

"I suggest that one or two of you take the positions of president and chairman."

"Not me. I don't want the responsibility," Sparkman said quickly.

Richmond looked directly at him. "As I mentioned earlier, I'm not part of the Office of General Counsel, but you already have responsibility for Dawn, Mr. Sparkman. However, any effort to improve the situation here, I would think, will be looked upon as a positive."

The room was quiet.

"You don't need to make a decision today, gentlemen. As I mentioned, your staff can generally operate on its own.

"However, one or more of you should meet with the current senior officers and give them some kind of guidance; and, in turn, ask for their ideas."

The room was again quiet.

"I have to go," Richmond said. "Do you have any more questions?"

He looked around to each of the individuals at the table. No one commented.

"If you have any questions after you digest the situation, please call me in Atlanta.

"The most important thing to remember is that this is still your company. You have employees, customers, and stockholders, and you're responsible to all of them."

With that final comment, he got up, picked up his briefcase, and walked out the door.

Several of the board members stood up.

"Since we're all here anyway, let's talk about this for a few minutes," Cohen said.

"I'm worn out," Adamson answered.

"We really need to make some decisions, guys; whether we want to or not," Cohen continued.

"Well, let's get on with it then," Sparkman said. He started to pace in the back of the room.

"I don't believe we should waste our time trying to find a CEO," Cohen started. "The chances of getting a top-notch person to accept this position are slim.

"Even if we could, there's no guarantee that he could alleviate our problems, and he'd cost us an arm and a leg."

"So where are you going with this, Arnie?" Sparkman asked.

Cohen spoke slowly, but definitively.

"I would like to nominate Alan Adamson as our interim chairman and president."

"Arnie, I...," Adamson said, starting to argue.

"Wait, let me finish.

"No one on this board has worked harder or questioned more. No one is any more devoted to Dawn or has been involved in generating the good will in the communities we service. And no one in this room has balls quite as brassy as Alan."

"That's for sure. He does have brass balls," Sparkman mumbled.

"What about it, Alan?" Cohen asked.

"I don't know. I don't think I can take it, physically."

Sparkman stopped his pacing, and looked at Adamson. "You're as strong as an ox, and you know it."

Adamson twisted around in his seat to see Sparkman.

"What happened to that adversarial role you took earlier. You hated my guts then?"

"I reevaluated the situation."

"I bet you did, you asshole. You just don't want the job."

"You're the asshole."

"Hey, guys! What are we doing here?" Cohen interrupted. "We've got horrendous problems—we need to work together."

Sparkman looked apologetic.

"Look, Alan, I'm sorry for the way I acted."

He turned and started walking in the other direction.

"Besides," He said quietly, but loud enough for all in the room to hear, "you probably wouldn't do a good job anyway."

"What did you say?" Adamson said, raising his voice.

"Nothing. I was just thinking out loud."

"Yeah. Well, kiss my ass!"

"I'll take the positions—both of them," Adamson said, glaring at Sparkman.

"Then I make a motion to appoint Alan Adamson to the positions of interim chairman and president of the board of Dawn Savings," Cohen said.

"I second that motion," Ed Marks added.

"All in favor, say aye."

All responded.

"All opposed?"

The room was silent.

"The vote is unanimous. Congratulations, Alan."

"Hello."

"Honey, it's me," Bill said.

"So how'd the meeting go? Like you thought it would?"

"Ron's gone?"

"Gone where?"

"Gone—he was let go today."

Marie said nothing. All Bill could hear was her controlled

breathing—something she always did when she tried not to cry.

"Honey, I don't think I'm going to have a problem. They need me," Bill said, trying to convince himself as much as Marie.

"But how do you know?" she cried. "You said that you didn't think Ron did anything wrong."

"I know," was all he could say.

Chapter 16

"Holy shit!" Jake Fleshman said, holding his head.

"So what's up?" Larry responded halfheartedly, still analyzing several volume and price charts.

"Ron Jameson resigned."

Larry swung around in his chair and looked at his brother.

"Did I hear you right?"

"You did. And Dawn had to sign a supervisory agreement, related to their acquisition, development, and construction portfolio."

"Pull up their price screen."

"I'm already there. They're at $7.25 and dropping."

Larry fell on his knees, raising his arms and his eyes upward.

"There truly is a God!" he screamed. "And he loves me!"

He got to his feet and put his hand on his brother's shoulder, who was focused on the news screen.

"Anything else?"

"Not yet."

"Call Norton-Steele. We'll do it one more time."

"You sure that we shouldn't just deliver and stay out? We've made a couple million already. Maybe they'll pull it out."

"Jake, did I convince you to get into Dawn?"

"Yes, you did."

"Have I been wrong on it yet?"

"No, you haven't."

"Then don't give me any shit," Larry responded, grinning.

"They'll never pull this one out, and I want to squeeze every fucking dollar I can out of this market. This is a terminal short, if I ever saw one. Let's go for it."

Jake picked up the telephone, looked at his brother and grinned. "I'm with you."

"You two are wearing me out," Alan Adamson said to Bill Casey and Lydia Lewis.

"Meeting with the lending department was a positive move," Lydia said. "Your spending the time to answer questions and to visit with them has really improved their morale."

"You think so?"

"I know so. Several of them were ready to walk out the door, and I can tell, that's not where they're at anymore.

"This afternoon we'll be meeting with five candidates for the workout position," Lydia continued.

"What did you think of the resumes, Bill?" Adamson asked.

"On paper, Arlie Winchester looks the best. Fortunately, I know several people who've had dealings with him. He's highly regarded."

"Good. I hope this won't be a long and drawn-out process."

"Maybe we'll get lucky," Lydia responded, putting her arm around Adamson.

"You're doing a good job, Chief."

"Thanks. I really wish we could do something significant for this company. I just don't feel like we're getting very far."

"A long journey is completed one step at a time," Bill said, winking.

"I know. I just have to keep reminding myself of that."

"By the way, Bill, you need to start spending even more time in New York. Considering our problems, I don't know how successful we'll be, but I'd like you to do everything possible to raise some capital or find a buyer."

"I've already started contacting some of the people I know, and you're right, it's going to be an uphill battle. If anything begins to look promising, I may need you up there with me."

"Just tell me when, and I'll be there. How's everything else going?"

"We should send out letters to all our customers who have over one hundred thousand dollars deposited with us, reminding them of the insurance limits," Lydia responded.

"That's kind of fatalistic, isn't it?"

"Maybe so," Bill interjected, "but necessary. No one knows when the regulators will decide to come in and take over. We can't put our customers at risk. Having capital alone may not be enough to keep them out."

"I still don't understand that," Adamson responded, moving his chair closer to the desk. "I thought that was the whole reason for intervention—a lack of net worth."

"If the government determines that the company is being operated in an 'unsafe and unsound' manner, it's over. And the definition of unsafe and unsound is a bit nebulous."

"But, we're working our asses off to do what's right," He answered.

"That's true, but because of the problems with our portfolio and conditions beyond our control, our delinquencies will continue to rise. And that's difficult for the regulators to accept," Bill said.

"Because Congress is all over their collective asses," Adamson said.

"That's right. And believe me, no matter what they do, there'll be a lot of Monday morning quarterbacking on Capitol Hill."

Adamson took a deep breath. "So what's the answer?" he asked.

"We need to continue to do what we're doing and keep the regulators informed. And make sure that our efforts are documented—we need that protection, and so do they."

"Fine, so we send letters out. Lydia, can you draft something up for me to sign?"

"It's already in process," she responded, smiling confidently. "And our savings branch managers need to reinforce that with the customers they come in contact with in their offices—on a person-to-person basis."

"Okay," Adamson acquiesced, shaking his head.

"Bill, can't we drop our rates to cut our losses? I'm getting a lot of criticism from our board. They know what others are paying, they know what our losses are, and they can't understand why Dawn's rates are at a premium. For that matter, neither can I."

"I've been trying to ratchet them down, but we have to be very careful. We're on a tightrope. If we drop too quickly, we could put ourselves in a real box."

"How so?"

"Well, since we're losing a considerable amount of money right now from operations, the only cash we have available to keep the doors open is from net savings increases. Without that growth, it's all over. We could be out of cash with nowhere to go for more.

"We're going to lose some savings automatically with our effort to eliminate the uninsured depositors, but that's a step we have to take to protect our customers."

"What about the government? I thought they'd protect us in serious cash situations like this," Adamson said, raising his voice.

"Not necessarily. Advances are made by the Federal Home Loan Bank system, and since its shareholders are other financial institutions, they're not interested in throwing money into a big black hole. Besides, we don't have any more good loans to use as collateral.

"So, we're in a catch-22?" He leaned across the desk, his eyes fixed on Bill.

"At minimum, we're in a very difficult position."

Adamson slammed the top of the desk with his open hand.

"God-damn it!" He said, standing up and starting to pace around the room, breathing heavily.

"So, we lose our balance on this tightrope, and the government steps in and tries to run it. Do they have the experience necessary to turn this thing around?"

"Generally, no they don't," Bill answered.

"So, if they trust us, and we have the experience, why don't they help, instead of sitting like vultures and waiting for us to die?"

Without giving Bill an opportunity to respond, Adamson continued.

"Ron worked with Hideo at Old Cyprus, and look what's happening—he just may pull it out. Why don't they give us the same chance?"

"That's not the way it works. Their main focus is overseeing smooth operations. If that's not happening, they have to protect their backsides, recognizing and accepting casualties, and the fact that life's not always fair," Bill said.

"Then why in the hell don't we just give up—admit that we've been put into a situation that's impossible to repair?"

"Because we don't know that yet, and it's our obligation to the shareholders and to our fellow citizens to play out our hand.

"Bottom line—we assumed some pretty hefty responsibilities when we took our positions with Dawn. For a number of reasons, we have problems and now our asses are on the line."

Adamson walked back to his desk and fell back into his chair.

"I just pray to God that we can all handle this pressure, mentally and physically," He said, looking worn and exhausted.

"We'll survive if we all work together," Lydia said.

Bill looked at his watch. "Time for our first interview. That's our cue to change our attitude to positive and exciting."

"God," Adamson said, laying his head in his arms on the desk. "Where's my white flag?"

Both Bill Casey and Alan Adamson looked like zombies on their flight back from New York.

Bill had spent a significant amount of time in Manhattan over the last several months, trying to interest any one of the large investment banking houses to work with Dawn in its effort to avoid catastrophe. The thrift needed a large capital injection if it expected to stay independent. On the other hand, he was convinced that any thought of an independent company vanished some time ago. The other alternative was selling Dawn. Any price would allow the stockholders to walk away with something.

He'd visited with Goldman Sachs, Solomon, Merrill, First Boston, and several others. Naturally, all were hesitant to be associated with a company that was still losing money, had questionable assets, and almost no chance of survival. Having the acting chairman and president with him was his final push to obtain some kind of commitment, but no luck.

"Alan," Bill said, looking straight ahead, "I want to tell you that I appreciate all the support you've given me since I've been at Dawn. And your leadership—you had a lot of chutzpah taking on the president and chairman's positions in the face of a pretty dismal outlook. I respect you a great deal for that."

Adamson looked over at Bill. "What brought that on?"

"Well," Bill said, hesitating slightly and closing his eyes. "I think we're at the end of the line."

"So we weren't successful on this trip. We'll try again."

"No, I don't think so," Bill said, opening his eyes and turning toward his boss and friend.

"While you were in the bathroom before we took off, I called the office to have someone pick us up when we arrive. There wasn't any answer."

"What do you mean there wasn't any answer? It's Friday afternoon. You're tired and you probably dialed the wrong number."

"No," He said, taking a deep breath. "I tried again. Still nothing. Then, just on a hunch, I called the Federal Home Loan Bank of Atlanta to talk to any one of the people we've been dealing with."

"And?"

"They were all unavailable."

"You think they're at Dawn?"

"Yes, I do."

Adamson sat back in his seat and shook his head. "If that's the case, we did everything we could."

"I guess. It's just very difficult for me. Dawn is an unbelievable organization in many ways—very positive and forward thinking. A number of us worked hard for that, but that won't be what people remember. It's sad," He said, closing his eyes.

Bill and Alan took a cab to Dawn's Boca headquarters. The parking lot was full of rental cars, and the intervention by the regulators was obvious. Through the windows, both Bill and Adamson could see unfamiliar men and women wandering in and out of the offices. As they walked up to the entrance near the executive wing, a stranger with a government badge attached to his suit coat opened the door, just enough for a conversation.

"Can I help you?"

"I'm Alan Adamson, the chairman and president of Dawn, and this is Bill Casey, the chief financial officer. We're on our way to our offices."

The stranger pushed the door open, allowing them to enter.

"This company has been put into conservatorship and no longer functions as a financial institution. There are no more directors, stockholders, or officers, for that matter," He said.

"So what happens to all this?" Adamson asked?

"On Monday morning, a new federal mutual company, Dawn Federal Savings, will begin functioning here. Positions will be appropriately assigned to some of Dawn's employees," he responded, as he checked a list on a clipboard. "You are both to see Mr. John Richmond. He's in that office to your left."

"That's my office!" Adamson answered tersely, obviously not completely in tune with what was happening.

"Come on," Bill said, putting his hand on Adamson's shoulder.

The room was full of men and women who looked much the same as one another. *They have got to be clones*, Bill thought.

John Richmond looked up and saw his two new arrivals, then glanced back at his staff.

"Ladies and gentlemen, can you give me a few minutes? And please close the door.

"Come on in, guys; have a seat."

"Thanks," Bill responded, straight-faced.

Adamson didn't comment.

"You knew it was coming," Richmond said.

"Sure we knew, but I thought we had more time," Adamson answered, irritably.

"We gave you as much time as we could. I know it probably won't make you two feel any better, but what you've tried to do over the last several months is very positive, and we appreciate your work."

"You're right, I don't feel any better," Adamson said.

"What happens to the employees and directors? The fellow at the door told us that there were no directors, officers, or shareholders."

"That's right. On Monday, Dawn will no longer be a state-chartered stock company; it will become a federally-chartered mutual association.

"New directors have already been asked to serve — in fact, they're here this evening. None of the current directors, including you Mr. Adamson, will be on the new board."

"I thought you said you appreciated what I did over the last several months."

"We do, but the policy isn't flexible."

"So I'm finished?"

"That's right. I'm sorry."

"So am I. What about the personal things I have in this office?"

"We'll have them boxed up and sent out to you."

"What about Bill?"

Richmond looked over at Bill with a slight smile.

"I would like him to stay on and help us work out the problems we have, if he's amenable. Based upon everyone we've talked to, and all the documentation we've read, he's done his best here in a very difficult environment."

"Can I let you know tomorrow?" Bill asked, looking exhausted.

"Sure."

"Are we free to leave?" Bill continued. "We're both very tired."

"Yes, but we'd like you here over the weekend to help us out, no matter what your decision."

"Sure," Bill said, with a forced smile.

"Marie."

"Yes."

"It's Lydia."

"Hi," Marie responded, hesitating. "Where's Bill? Is he okay?"

"He's fine, but..."

"But what?"

"The regulators took over the company today."

"Where are you?"

"I'm home, and Bill should be on his way soon. I saw him and Alan pulling in the parking lot, but I couldn't talk to anyone at that point. And I just wanted to go home."

"Did they leave you both go?" Marie asked, hesitantly.

"No. They really need help and said there'll be plenty of work to do if we were interested in staying."

Marie took a deep breath. "I appreciate the call," She said weakly.

"Are you okay?" Lydia asked.

"Sure—it's just difficult. You know that I never really wanted Bill to leave Palm Savings. It took me a long time to adjust to that decision."

"I can only imagine, Marie. But he really tried to turn this company around. It was just too far gone. And Nick being around as long as he was, made the challenge even more difficult."

Marie took a deep breath. "I know. Thanks for calling. I appreciate your friendship. We both do."

Chapter 17

Friday evening at Jake Fleshman's house was festive, with streamers, lanterns, party hats, and champagne. The pleasant aroma of steaks on the grill hung in the air, and there was a buffet table filled with corn-on-the-cob, baked potatoes, watermelon, and other foods. The party had been quickly called after the takeover was announced on the wire late Friday afternoon. The pool and deck were filled with business associates and friends.

Larry and Jake were recapping their position in the latter's den before they joined the festivities.

"What a call," Larry said, grinning at his brother.

"What do you think the stock will come out at on Monday?" Jake asked.

"I'm not sure—probably somewhere around twenty-five cents a share, but it really doesn't matter."

"Why? Since we've never done a financial institution before, or any company for that matter that's this close to the end of the line, I don't understand the modus operandi."

"Well, I didn't either, but I did some homework and it is a little different with a financial institution, but the result is generally the same as with any failed company."

"Explain."

"I'd say that the stock will go to zero immediately, but there are always a few people out there, real risk-takers, that think the government will work out some kind of deal with the current management and stockholders."

"But you don't think so?"

"No way. They'll get whatever's left after they sell the assets and payoff the liabilities—nothing. Any play in the stock will disappear when the Street understands that no deals of any kind have been reached."

"So, you're saying that the end result is the terminal short we talked about—we don't even have to buy back in."

"You got it," Larry responded, with a broad grin.

"How about some champagne?"

"I thought you'd never ask."

Larry put his arm around his brother and they walked out to the pool deck toward the drinks, snacks and festivities.

Telling Marie is probably more difficult than actually losing the company, Bill thought, as he slowly drove home. *So now where's my career? Nowhere.*

Then he saw her standing in the driveway. *Why would she be out there? Does she know?*

Bill slowly got out of his car and looked at her. Marie's eyes were wet and red. He put his arms around her and held her close.

"I'm sorry honey. It just didn't work out."

"I know. Lydia called."

It was difficult for him to speak. "I know I let you down."

She moved away from him slightly and looked into his eyes. "You did what you thought was right. They're keeping you on for a time, and that's good. You'll find something—we'll be okay."

Bill knew that Marie didn't really believe what she was saying, and he loved her even more for saying it.

"I appreciate your time. If we need you to testify, we'll call you," said Kurt Schneider, Assistant U.S. District Attorney, as he showed his sixty-eighth potential witness out the door.

The investigation had not gone well. By allowing Carr and Larson to overdraw their checking account by millions of dollars, there was no question that a federal law was violated.

The sale of the hotel in Coconut Grove by the same parties to Dawn for much more than their purchase, in less than a year, with all profits going to pay delinquent interest on their other loans and a large overdraft was an obvious sham transaction, and also criminal.

On the other hand, even if a Grand Jury could be convinced, there would be competition in the subsequent trial.

Without significant evidence, a smart defense lawyer could be successful with a defense of "poor business judgment", or something similar. Jameson needed to be shown as the true leader, with everyone else following his direction into oblivion.

Schneider needed believable witnesses who would help him get there.

"Hey, Kurt. How's it hangin?" Mike Vilon said as he entered the room and slapped Schneider on the shoulder.

Vilon was an examiner from the FHLBB who had been assigned to the case full time. Because of his experience on the Dawn exam and his knowledge of the company and its management, he was asked to assist the Department of Justice in its effort to indict Jameson.

Schneider looked up. "Not real great. I have to show that Jameson was in complete control, and the people I talked to so far haven't given me any help.

"Over and above him, there were evidently several strong personalities inside and outside the bank that affected its' direction. He sure as hell wasn't a dictator."

"So what are you trying to say?" Vilon asked.

Schneider was happy to get some assistance on the case, but Vilon was as dense as a rock. Schneider slowly moved his chair around so that he was looking directly at Vilon, now sitting on the edge of his desk.

He spoke slowly, and the volume of his voice increased with each word.

"It means I'm going to lose another case. And get off my desk!"

Vilon got up and bent over the desk, looking directly at Schneider.

"Listen, you're the big time assistant prosecutor. Don't get all over my ass because you don't think you have a case. I'll talk to my supervisor and get out of here tomorrow."

He started to walk out of the office, and Schneider got up and grabbed him by the arm.

"Listen, Mike, I'm sorry, okay? This is a very difficult case, and I need you to help me come up with a direction."

Vilon swung around and looked at Schneider. "I accept your apology, but don't give me any more of your shit."

Schneider raised his eyebrows at Vilon sheepishly.

"Agreed. Sit down and help me think this thing through."

Vilon walked over to one of the guest chairs and slowly sat down.

"What do you think we need to do in order to get the jury to believe us and get him convicted?" Schneider asked.

"We need internal and external witnesses in prominent positions who will swear to his control, to his unwavering position to do things his way."

Schneider stopped, leaned back in his chair and stared at the ceiling.

"And that he took advantage of people through his position at Dawn, along the way—that would cinch it."

"What about his senior officers? Any potential there?"

"I doubt it. They're all different, but I get the impression that they have one thing in common."

"What's that?"

"They all believe that Ron did what he did to buy time; to salvage whatever he could."

Schneider shook his head. "Well, that won't help us. We want to send him to the slammer, not proclaim him a saint."

"Exactly. So, who do we have on the outside? You know more about that potential."

"Carr and Larson are our only options."

"Impossible!" Vilon said. "For God's sake, we're after them, too."

Schneider cocked his head to the side and raised his eyebrows, slyly.

"What are you suggesting? Put pressure on them about potential indictment and then make them a deal?"

Schneider smiled.

Vilon jumped out of his chair, leaning over Schneider's desk.

"You're not serious? Those two have done as much to put Dawn in the tank as anyone—probably more. We both know that they lie and cheat—and Larson-he's totally screwed up."

Schneider said nothing.

Vilon started to pace around the room.

"Number one," he continued, "how are you going to convince the jury that they're credible? And number two,

Jameson's probably more innocent than your proposed witnesses."

He stopped and looked directly at Schneider.

"We can't find credible witnesses to help us convince the jury that there's been significant wrongdoing, so we ask these two jerk-offs to lie for us? How can you even suggest this approach?"

"Who said they're going to lie?"

"You've got to be shitting me, Kurt. They'll know what we want to hear, and it won't be the truth. You know it, and I know it."

Schneider quietly sat listening to Vilon.

"Kind of self-righteous, aren't you, Mike?"

Before giving him an opportunity to comment, Schneider continued.

"What license do you have dictating the type of legal system we should use in this country? What we have available is something that's evolved over a lot of years. And you know what—it works."

Vilon was quiet and straight-faced.

"Yes, maybe they will lie, but that's not my problem. Once we get to trial, it's up to the jury to decide whether they're credible after questioning by the defense.

"This may shock you, but I don't care whether Jameson is innocent or guilty. I'm on the prosecution side, and that's what I aim to do—prosecute—no matter what it takes. If the system is working properly and he's not guilty, he'll be found innocent. If he is, he won't."

"So what happens if the system doesn't work and an innocent man is found guilty?"

"That's not my concern, but rather a shortcoming of his defense. If you can't accept that logic, I really don't need your help. I have no other direction to go."

Vilon said nothing.

"I've got work to do," Schneider said, as he gathered some of his work on the desk and walked out the door and down the hallway.

Vilon and Schneider walked into the latter's office.

"I never thought it would end," Schneider said, running his hand through his sweaty, thinning hair.

"I didn't either, but you got what you wanted. He's indicted, and now we need to start preparing for the trial."

"Right. Both Carr and Larson have agreed to testify, and that's good."

"I guess."

"I've also convinced Doug Carson to testify for us."

"Doug Carson—you're not serious?"

Schneider winced. "We've talked about this before. If you don't have the stomach for it, get out. I'll do it on my own. I feel comfortable with the direction I'm taking."

Vilon shook his head, and walked out the door.

The jury reentered the courtroom, and Marie squeezed Bill's hand. Even before the guilty verdict was read, Jameson's mother and wife started to cry. His father laid his face in his hands.

Ron had prepared his wife and parents for several guilty counts, with probably at least ten years to follow at the sentencing.

On hearing the words, he was expressionless. After hesitating, he took a deep breath, looked around and gave his family the smile they were so used to seeing. He turned toward his lawyer and extended his hand.

"Thanks, Pete. I know you did the best you could."

"Ron, we'll get them on appeal. No sweat."

Ron didn't respond. He just nodded and walked back toward his wife and parents.

"Mr. Jameson," one of the marshals called.

"Give me a break—just a few minutes," He said, as he leaned over the rail that separated the observers' section from the rest of the courtroom. Sara and his parents grabbed for him all at once, hugging him and each other tightly.

"Not to worry. Pete feels confident that we can win on appeal," He assured them.

Hideo Tabani was in the courtroom each day. His sister-club relationship in Japan was finalized, along with his reciprocity with the Vero Beach Club. These two developments and his marketing efforts were finally starting to pay off. Sales were picking up and his cash flow was steady.

"Andrew."

Stephen put his hand on Andrew's shoulder and shook it slightly.

"Andrew," He said, again.

Andrew looked at Stephen with a blank stare.

"The trial's over."

"I know. I heard," He said, looking up at Stephen.

"The problem is that no matter how many years he gets, he'll still get out. He deserves worse. He ruined too much for us!"

Andrew's obvious intensity concerned Stephen.

"I'm not going into this with you again. The guy's going to jail, and his family feels bad enough without you making comments that he's not being punished enough," Stephen whispered. "I'm leaving."

He turned and walked toward the aisle.

Mr. Jameson, Ron's father, broke slightly away from the emotional and physical hold of the family, to wipe his eyes when he noticed Schneider. As the prosecutor passed through the gate, he grabbed his coat.

"Look what you've done to my family. You're a waste to society."

Schneider tried to break away from the older man, but Mr. Jameson had a vice grip on his coat.

"Dad, don't bother with him. He's not worth it," Ron said, as he quickly moved through the gate toward his father.

Immediately two marshals moved toward their ward. They grabbed at Jameson as he tried to step between his father and Schneider.

"You son-of-a-bitch, you ruined us!" Andrew yelled as he moved closer, pointing a small pistol at Jameson.

"You're a dead man!"

"Don't, Andrew!" Stephen yelled. He tried to grab Larson's arm, but he only slightly grazed it.

It all happened too quickly. The shot rang out. Almost immediately, in one swift movement, the gun was separated from Larson, and he was thrown to the floor by one of the marshals, handcuffed, and read his rights.

Bill was just beginning to feel the intensity of the morning heat as he pounded on the neighborhood streets. He was listening to Harry Chapin sing *Circle* on his headphones.

His mind flashed back to that last day of the Jameson trial—the shooting and the blood. The headline, "ASSISTANT PROSECUTOR—MURDERED IN COURTROOM," was in every paper in South Florida, and on television and radio throughout the nation.

He was nearing the end of his run and he started to sprint, trying to use that last burst of energy he had in his body. His mind was moving as fast as his torso—maybe faster.

I'm sure that those of us who were involved with the new breed of financial institutions learned something from the experience, he thought, *but it'll be forgotten. As human beings, we're terrible students of history—even our own. We repeat and repeat our errors after the ego and power replace logic.*

Harry Chapin continued to sing, "All my life's a circle, sunrise and sundown...it seems like I been here before, I can't remember when. But I got this feeling that I'll be back once again."

God give me the strength, he thought, cooling down as he walked back to his house.

994009

Made in the USA